The Cowboy's Housekeeper

clean & wholesome at it's best

Lori Copeland

This is a work of fiction. All the characters, organizations, and events portrayed are either products of the author's imagination or are used fictitiously.

The Cowboy's Housekeeper

Edited by Virginia Smith

Cover by Sweet 'N Spicy Designs

ISBN-13: 978-0-9854923-7-3
ISBN-10: 0-9854923-7-6

One

The sound of a crowing rooster filtered through the thin shears hanging at Jessica Cole's childhood bedroom window. Jessica nestled between the light blanket, smelling of sunshine and Tide. She drowsily opened her eyes to see the faint streaks of dawn breaking over the horizon. Her gaze scanned the familiar room, pausing on the small photograph sitting on her dressing table. The clear images of Uncle Fred, Aunt Rainey, and herself as a child smiled back at her. Tears momentarily welled to her eyes. For a second time this year the phone had rung in the middle of the night to summon her home.

Aunt Rainey had followed Uncle Fred so swiftly in

death that the fact made Jessica's head spin. A brief six months ago she was home to help her aunt bury Uncle Fred under that same old spreading oak where they laid Aunt Rainey to rest two short days earlier.

Sighing, she turned on her side, the faint light in the room growing ever brighter.

One fact stood out clearly. Fred and Rainey had been well loved in this small Texas community. The love surrounding her the morning of her aunt's funeral left no doubt the town felt the loss as much as she. She sat at the small grave site, her gaze roaming familiar faces. When her aunt and uncle opened their home to her as the child they were never able to have, the people of this town became part of her life. Just like Fred and Rainey, they opened their arms to a four-year-old orphan whose parents had just died in a boating accident.

She could still hear Aunt Rainey's weak voice, two days before her death. "You were ours as surely as if I had given birth to you myself. Fred and I were never blessed with the children we wanted," she whispered in a tired voice. "Not that the Lord hasn't been real good to us." Her eyes had taken on a soft, misty look as she continued. "Each other was enough—for a while, but I've thanked the good Lord every day for you. There's something special about a child in a person's life. Makes them less selfish, able to think of others more readily. So, when God seen fit to send you to us, well...you've been a blessing, Jessie and we loved you."

"Oh, Aunt Rainey," Jessica whispered. "I love both of you so much." She couldn't imagine a life without this woman to confide in, to lend hope when life got complicated. And life did have a way of getting complicated.

She shifted beneath the sheets, her mind unwillingly returning to the tall man who had stood to the left of the old tree, his hat in his hand, his head bowed. The sun glistened brightly on thick golden-brown hair. And like the young schoolgirl that once loved him with every ounce of her being, her heart dropped to her stomach. Would there ever come a time when she could look at Jason Rawlings without remembering....

He stood exactly a chin-length above her. Tall enough that she was forced to stand on her toes to kiss him—small price at the time. In contrast to his mist-green summer shirt, his skin held the warm tan of a man who spent a lot time outdoors. The shirt went well with his western-cut suit. Broad, straight shoulders—had he bulked up since she last saw him?—and a solid wall chest tapered down to a lean waist and slim hips.

There should be a law against a man looking that good.

It would be her luck for him to show up that morning. Good fortune hadn't exactly frequented Jessica's life lately. Her gaze traveled slowly back to Jason Rawlings, and she blushed as his brilliant jade-green eyes locked with hers. She quickly lowered her gaze to the casket and the large floral tribute she'd ordered two days earlier. Daisies. Aunt Rainey loved daisies and there were three dozen multi-colored blooms to accompany her into eternity.

When the mourners broke up, soft voices greeted others. Several old-time acquaintances stopped by her chair to offer condolences, a gentle pat on the arm and words of comfort. Pastor Franklin stepped to her side, taking her arm as they walked slowly toward the long black limousine waiting at the side of the county road.

Jessica's good-byes had been said at the funeral home the night before. Now it was a matter of getting to the car and driving away.

Somehow the brief ceremony didn't seem to be enough for all Aunt Rainey had given her, but Rainey didn't want a fuss made. Her soft last words ran through Jessica's mind. "Hate those long drawn out good-bye's. No big, sad service. Just bury me next to papa.'"

Jessica looked back at the light-gray casket one final time. Drawing a deep breath, she turned and walked on.

Moments later the long black car had pulled out of the cemetery onto the dusty road.

❦

This morning, the sun had come up as usual. Life went on. Jessica piled out bed and shuffled to the kitchen. The old house was falling apart; everything needed fixing—the roof, the plumbing, the windows. In order to sell the place, she would price the land, and insist the house be included.

Spooning grinds into the old coffee pot filter—Jessica noticed the new Keurig coffee system she'd sent Rainey for Christmas was still in its box in the pantry—she then filled the pot with water, set the basket in the pot and placed the aluminum relic on the gas burner. Striking a match, she touched the fire to the jet, and sprang back when fire exploded. Her fingers flew up to search for eyebrows. Still intact, thank goodness. Adjusting the flame, she realized her mind was still on Rainey's graveside service. Of course, a member of the Rawlings family would be in attendance, despite that one crazy incident eight years ago. Jason hadn't attended Uncle Fred's funeral, but his mother had come. The Cole property adjoined his parents'. Before the incident eight years earlier the two neighbors had been good friends.

Those were good years. Really, good years. She'd had a crush on Jason Rawlings from the day she laid eyes on him. Her was six and she'd been around four. She'd given him a toad she'd caught near the well house. He'd taken it. From that day on she'd tagged after him, constantly under his feet. In turn, he bugged the daylights out of her. Grade school to high school, her heart leaped to her throat every time he rode over to talk business with Uncle Fred or to pay a visit to Aunt Rainey's kitchen, where his favorite pie or cake always seemed to be cooling on Rainey's kitchen windowsill.

Shaking memories aside, she headed to the old bath, dreading the thought of another cold shower. The water heater wasn't working properly. It ran tepid water that quickly reverted to well house cold if one lingered.

There would be endless paperwork to fill out, death certificates to distribute. The Rainey's personal affects needed to be sorted and given away. The old car, truck and tractor wouldn't bring much, but they would have to be disposed of. She'd have to stop by Afton Asher's Realtor to list the farm and land, soon. Ashton would be delighted. The old coot had wanted to get his hands on this farm for years. Why, Jessica couldn't imagine, except the acreage with its several spring-fed ponds and good grazing grass was well known in the area.

She left the kitchen. Might as well face the cold shower and get it over with.

The experience should be a great start to another perfectly miserable day.

Two

The sun still hung low in the morning sky when Jessica wrestled Uncle Fred's rusty old truck down the gravel driveway on her way to town. This thing should have been replaced a decade ago, but Uncle Fred refused. "We've got college expenses coming up," he'd say. "Why spend good money on a new one when this one works just fine?"

Well, it *didn't* work just fine. The gearshift lever took two hands to shove, and the gas pedal stuck. Besides, on a day like today some air conditioning would be nice.

By the time she parked in front of the Baker's house, her hair stuck to her neck and her makeup rolled off her face with drops of perspiration.

Wilma Baker opened the door, giving Jessica a wide

smile. Uncle Fred always said

Wilma's fanny looked like two wildcats wrestling in a gunnysack. Unkind, but true.

"Jessica Cole, come in here girl and let me look at you." Wilma beamed. "Gracious me, you're prettier than ever! I told the judge this morning, why you hadn't run off to Hollywood to be one of them big movie stars is beyond me. Mercy sakes, Fred and Rainey was proud of you!"

Jessica's cheeks warmed at the outlandish praise. Steering the conversation into another channel, she asked, "I'm not too early?"

"Heavens to Betsy, child, not if you don't mind waiting until the judge finishes his lunch. He won't be long now. Come in, sweetie, you can wait in his study." She proceeded to lead the way through the comfortable old living room. The clock on the mantle was chiming and Edna's birds were singing in cages hanging in the front window.

They moved down the hall and paused in front of a large oak door. Wilma poked her head into the room and then motioned for Jessica to enter.

"Now, you just make yourself at home. The judge will be with you in a bit." Jessica sank into the overstuffed chair in front of the judge's desk. Wilma patted her shoulder and then closed the door behind her, leaving Jessica to rediscover the room. She sat with her hands in her lap, gaze roaming down the long line of certificates hanging on the wall. She paused on Justice of the Peace. Judge Baker had married her and Jason that one special night....

"Married!" Aunt Rainey, dressed in her nightgown and robe, had sunk weakly into the chair at the kitchen table when the young couple announced their news.

"Well, I won't hear of it," Uncle Fred boomed out, his loud, deep voice echoing the room.

Jessica had sought the comfort of Jason's arm, panic filling her. She had never dreamed they would take the news this badly. They loved Jason!

"Merciful heavens, boy. What in the world were you thinking?" Fred drew an exasperated breath. "She's nothing but a child!" His features turned scarlet and his breath came in heavy rasps. "She's not ready to take on the responsibility of a marriage."

"I know she's young, sir." Jason held tight to Jessica's trembling hand. "But that doesn't change anything. We plan for her to complete school and go to college."

"Jessica, dear, you can't handle both." Aunt Rainey pleaded, her pale eyes full of tears. "Marriage is a scared commitment—and college? Why, you'll need every moment to study if you ever want to become a veterinarian."

Jessica had never felt so low. Or guilty. She was fully aware of Rainey and Fred's dream for her. They never had an education, and for years they talked of nothing else for Jessica. It was as if they sought to relive their life through her.

Jason shifted, his gaze searching Jessica's.

"The marriage will have to be annulled." Uncle Fred sank wearily into his chair, his features pale and ashen. Moonlight streamed through the lace curtain.

"Fred, take your medicine," Aunt Rainey said between tears. She got up apparently to get the amber-colored bottle from the shelf.

Jason spoke. "I'm sorry, sir, but Jesse and I love each other. I can't allow you annul the marriage."

"You don't have a darn thing to say about it, son. She's under age." The elderly man popped one of the tiny white pills Wilma handed him under his tongue. "I can't let you destroy something we dreamed of and worked for all our life. You're a fine man, Jason. I have no qualms about you as a person. I've known you all your life, but I'll move heaven and earth to get this marriage set aside—annulled—whatever it takes. You can trust my word on that that. Jessica!"

Jessica snapped to attention, her heart feeling as though it were being torn in half. "Yes, Uncle Fred?"

"Go to your room. I'll handle things from here on out."

Jessica glanced at Jason, tears filling her eyes. "Uncle Fred, I love him . . ."

"I said go to your room, girl!" he roared.

"Jessica." Jason's voice stopped her. "Stay here. Don't leave. Somehow we'll work this thing out together." His beautiful green eyes reflected pools of living torment.

"I'm sorry, Jason. It's out of your hands," Fred said. "Now go home and we'll forget this night ever happened."

Rainey reached for Jessica's hand. "Come with me, dear. Let your Uncle take care of this matter."

"No!" Jessica broke away. "Leave us alone—all of you. Leave us alone! We know what we want."

Uncle Fred gasped sharply and all eyes focused on him.

"Fred!" Rainey stepped to support his frame when he grasped his arm. Her eyes met Jessica's. "Please," she begged, "do as he says." The lines in her face filled with pain and worry.

Jason's voice turned tense. "I don't want to do anything to jeopardize Fred's health. We'll take this up in the morning. Jessica, call an ambulance."

"Go home." Fred roared. "And stay there. Jessica is under age and you're not wanted here."

"Jason." Jessica reached for his hand. "Maybe you'd better go home. I'll call you later."

"No. I'll stay with you. We'll get Fred to the hospital..."

"Jason, don't make me choose between you and them." How could she choose between breaking Uncle Fred and Aunt Rainey's hearts, maybe bringing on a fatal heart attack in the process—and giving up the man she loved more than her own life? The decision would tear her apart.

Jason's jaw firmed. "If you make me, I'll go. But you need to think about the vows you took not an hour ago. You're young, but I will take care of you. I love you." His gaze met hers.

Fred reached out to grasp Jessica's hand. "Get me to the hospital, honey."

Her gaze switched from Fred to Jason. Jason to Fred. Rainey's tear-filled eyes.

Judging by the hardening of his jaw, Jason's patience with the situation was wearing thin. "If I walk out that door without you, there'll be no turning back. I know you're in a heck of a situation, but together we'll work through this."

Blinking to see through a watery veil, Jessica's gaze swept the faces in the room, Aunt Rainey's tear-streaked one, Uncle Fred's sickly gray one, her beloved Jason's. Death would be an easier choice for her at this moment.

"I.... can't leave Fred and Rainey right now." She prayed to God she was making the wise choice.

But it had been the worse choice she ever made.

Mist swelled to Jessica's eyes and she snatched a tissue from her purse. What was taking the judge so long? She drummed her fingertips on the arm of the old chair, staring at the wall in front of her, rapidly blinking back tears. She had no control over the memories or emotions that flooded her, and if she was ever going to get through the reading of the will, she would have to put the past firmly behind her.

She thought back to that black week before she left for college. Those days the worst in Jessica's life. Fred recovered from the "incident" and life settled back to normal. She waited for the phone to ring, for Jason to call, but he didn't. She spent hours staring at her cell phone, aching to call Jason to come after her. Every time she rejected the idea. She had bruised his pride. A deep resentment toward her aunt and uncle filled her heart, and she looked forward to the day when she would board the bus for Austin and fulfill *their* dream of her becoming a vet.

Not hers.

Her mind returned to the present. Why cry over spilt milk? She had grieved for Jason for eight long years. The time had come—past time—to get on with her life.

The study door opened and Judge Baker's voice filled the air. "Well, well, if it isn't little Jessie Cole." He circled her chair and bent to place an affectionate peck on her cheek. Mrs. Baker stood beside him, smiling. He straightened and moved to stand behind his massive oak desk.

The years had been considerate. A thatch of snow white hair and eyes not quite the same bright hue, were the only touch time had given the man. His jaunty grin still had the impact of a youthful suitor.

"My, my." His eyes teased her with a twinkle. "What I wouldn't give to be thirty years younger right now. Mama, I must warn you. You'd be a fool to leave me alone with a pretty little dumpling like this one." He gave "Mama" a mischievous wink.

"Oh, go on with you, Daddy. If you were thirty years younger, you'd still be too old for her. But," Mama added, "I'd still be here."

He threw back his head and laughed. "No need to

worry. I've had you for fifty years. My eyes are blind."

"Horse patoot, you old goat." She laughed. "Go on with you. You'll scare this little thing to death. Now, you behave yourself. I've got a cake in the oven and haven't got time to stand around listening to your foolishness." She turned and gave the judge a saucy grin, along with some parting advice. "Just remember your age, Daddy, and your heart!"

He chuckled when the door closed with a resounding bang.

Taking a seat in the large leather chair behind his desk, he settled a benign gaze on Jessica.

"Jessie, dear"—his voice was so kind—"we are so sorry about your loss. And so close together." He shook his head sadly. "There wasn't a finer pair of people on earth as far as Mama and I were concerned." He stood and walked over to the window, gazing out at the street. "When you live to be Mama's and my age, it seems you spend half your time burying the people you love and have spent most of your life with."

He stood for a moment with a faraway look in his eyes—eyes that didn't quite have the brightness they used to have. With a slight shrug of his stooped shoulders he turned back to the business of living. He cleared his throat, shuffled through a short stack of papers lying before him, and began.

"My dear, this should basically be very simple. As you know, all Fred and Rainey had will be yours." He sat back down at his desk. For the first time Jessica could ever recall, he had a rather sheepish look on his face.

"There is only one small stipulation to the will that Fred and Rainey executed a few weeks before Fred graduated to Heaven." He glanced up at Jessica and continued. "I don't imagine you're going to care much for it."

Jessica couldn't imagine what the judge meant. She clutched the arms of the chair, bracing herself for what was to come.

He began to explain the details of the will. "Land, house, material possessions, etc., etc., all to go to you with the stipulation that you return to run the farm for six months. Make certain everything is disposed of properly or left in good hands, if you sell out. If you decide to return to Austin immediately, then the entire estate will be left to Manor Methodist Church, where, as you know, Fred and Rainey had been members for over fifty years."

Heat crept up her neck and sudden rage simmered within her. How dare they play God with her life again! She was an adult—perfectly capable of controlling her destiny. She jumped to her feet and stormed over to the large window that looked out on the main street. "How could they do it?" she demanded. "*Why* did they do it?"

"Why?" the judge said gently. "Because they loved you, Jessie. They simply could not stand the thought of you never coming back to the home and land they had loved. They have waited patiently all these years, hoping you'd return"—the judge cleared his throat before continuing—"and that you'd forgiven them. The matter of you and Jason weighed heavily on their minds—how they interfered when perhaps—just perhaps they shouldn't have."

"It should have," Jessica replied in a rare show of hurt feelings, "but they knew I had forgiven them." *Not really,* her heart cried. Not completely, but the past was forgotten. "How am I going to run that farm and my business at the same time? Ask me about fashion, and I can tell you anything you want to know. But farming? I know very little about manure and grain."

"Oh, right. Rainey said you had become quiet the entrepreneur. Ladies fancy jeans, isn't it?"

"Fancy Duds."

"Fancy Duds? My, my. I'll have to get Mama a pair."

Jessica caught back a laugh when the image of

Wilma flashed through her mind wearing the skin-tight denim with a row of sequins on the back pockets.

The idea for Fancy Duds was conceived in the dressing room of a department store in an Austin mall during her sophomore year at the university. Her roommates had roped her into a shopping trip to help Ginny Lou find an outfit for a date to her first rodeo. The hat, blouse, and boots had been easy to find, but jeans? Jessica and Barb sat outside the dressing room and critiqued each pair Ginny Lou tried.

"Ick, no." Barb scrunched her nose at a baggy pair.

Jessica agreed. "Looks like you could fit an elephant in there with you."

With an expansive eye-roll, Ginny Lou stomped back into the dressing room, only to appear a few minutes later wearing another pair.

"Hmmm." Barb tapped a finger against her lips as she examined the fit. "A possibility."

Jessica circled Ginny Lou, tugging at the waistband, fingering the side-seam. "These would work, but they're so..." She searched for a word. "Plain."

Barb's finger pointed at her. "Exactly. They're snug enough to hug your curves, but they do nothing to emphasize your best feature."

A cautious question appeared on Ginny Lou's face. "And that would be?"

Jessica exchanged a grin with Barb. "Your posterior, sweetie. What you need is some bling back here." She hooked a finger through the rear belt loop and tugged, an idea materializing. "You know what? I think I can come up with just the thing. A handful of glittery beads, a few rhinestone studs. And one of my—" She waved a hand expansively in the air with a grin full of bluster—"incredible designs."

"She's right," Barb agreed with a nod. "Her designs are amazing. This might be the perfect use for her doodles. Unless she wants to become a tattoo designer."

They all snorted with laughter.

"Okay." A smile curved Ginny Lou's mouth. "I'll buy these jeans and place them in your capable hands. Just make me look like a million bucks, okay?"

Those jeans had been the start of a craze that not only paid Jessica's way through college, but had begun to earn some real money in recent years. And Aunt Raney and Uncle Fred wanted her to put her business aside for six months to *run a farm*?

The judge shuffled a stack of papers on his desk, seeming to search for the right words. Finally, tossing the papers aside he said, "Fred suggested you hire Jason to do it."

"What?" Jessica's mouth gaped in shock.

"Now think about it for a minute, Jessica. The plan could make a whole lot of sense. Jason's one of the biggest ranchers around right now. His property adjoins yours, plus he's got the manpower to run both ranches. And—to tell you the truth, I don't know of another man around I would trust or even recommend doing the job for you."

Jessica stood in front of his wooden desk, speechless. Finally able to find her tongue, she said in a determined voice, "Even if I would think about anything that preposterous, Judge Baker, I'm sure Jason would laugh himself into a hysterical fit at the asinine suggestion. My gosh, you do realize we didn't exactly part best friends? "

"Oh, now, Jessica," the judge admonished laughingly, "that was a long time ago. You are two reasonable adults now, more than able to conduct a simple business arrangement—which is all this would be."

Jessica snorted in a very unladylike way. "Maybe Jason's wife wouldn't care for the suggestion."

"Wife? That boy hasn't married and settled down yet. I'd be surprised if he ever does." He shuffled the papers into a neat stack. "Now I've promised Rainey I'd help you through this time and I suggest you take a few days to think this over. As soon as you calm down, I'm sure you'll view the situation differently."

She jutted her chin forward. "I can say with certainty I don't want the farm. Give it to the church."

Though the older man's expression did not change, disapproval wafted off him in waves. "Very well. I will call and inform the church that everything Fred and Rainey worked and toiled all of their life to achieve will go to that establishment."

Jessica's firm lower jaw trembled. Long winters on the farm when Fred had waded in hip-deep snow to break ice to feed the cattle. Rainey fussing with the old washing machine because she didn't want to spend the money for a new one. "Jessie might need it," she would say. Fred did without a new truck in order to tuck a little aside, and Rainey wore the same old dresses to church for years. Giving all to the church was noble idea—so noble that Jessica liked the idea of honoring Rainey and Fred's thoughtfulness. But she had plans for that money. Once her new clothing line launched, she would donate a percentage of the profits to her aunt and uncle's church.

But she would *not* be manipulated!

"Fine."

"Fine." The judge glanced up. "If you change your mind, you'll let me know?"

She shouldered her purse and looked him in the eye. "I won't change my mind."

Three

As Jessica let herself out into the hot afternoon air, her mind was spinning in a thousand directions. What was she supposed to do now? Even if she had wanted to come home, even if she hated the big city, the traffic, the crime, the judge's suggestion was the principle of the thing! She had more money now than she ever dreamed. She didn't need the inheritance. But that farm was all Fred and Rainey had in life.

Now that her emotions had cooled, she realized her choice was fixed. She either did as the will stated and dealt with Mr. High and Mighty Rawlings or give away what Fred and Rainey worked all their lives to accomplish.

She literally stomped her foot in a fit of anger before climbing behind the wheel of the truck, still puffing inside. Why did *everything* have to be so complicated?

Swiping her eyes with the backs of her hands, she reached down to turn the key in the ignition. "Don't you give me any trouble. I'm not in the mood for it!" The old motor groaned to life reluctantly. She threw the gear shift into reverse and shot out of the driveway like a missile. That darn gas pedal! She struggled wildly to get the truck under control. To her mounting horror, the motor gave one long backfire, and with a surge of speed that left her breathless, careened out onto the street backward, heading straight toward one of the late-model pickups sitting idling in front of the feed store.

Jessica closed her eyes tight and jammed her foot on the brake. She felt the bone-jarring jolt and the sickening screech of bending metal as the truck came to an abrupt halt, sitting halfway through the side of the dark-blue pickup. She opened her eyes slowly and released a shaky breath. Not a sound could be heard for a few moments beyond a ringing in her ears as she sat there trying to gather her wits about her. Voices jarred her out of her paralyzed state as people around her started moving.

"My lordy, are you hurt, little lady?" cried Luther, a man who worked at the feed store. He added in an excited voice, "Boy, we can sure thank our lucky stars there was no one around this here truck just now. Why, when I looked up and saw you a flyin' out of that driveway like a bat out of hell—oh, pardon me, ma'am, but as I was saying, I looked up, and then I sez to ol' Jason, 'Man, someone's just bought you a new truck!'"

"Jason?" Oh, good heavens, that was all she needed. *Please, God, don't let this be his truck.* But the thought had barely left her mind when her eyes caught the figure of a tall, dark, ridiculously good-looking man striding toward her. He stopped directly in front of the front bumper and planted his hands on his slim hips. Taking one despairing look at his truck, he turned back around slowly and fixed his brilliant jade-green gaze on her.

Jessica smiled beguilingly as her words of long ago came back home to her. She had always vowed that someday she would make Jason Rawlings notice her again. Well, the day had arrived.

She tumbled out of the truck, her face feeling as red as a beet. How could she have hit *his* pickup when there were half-dozen others sitting around? By this time Jason was squatting on the ground, apparently trying to access the damage beneath his truck. Jessica could see clearly beneath the vehicle from where she stood, and she was sure he would not like what he saw. There were all kinds of odds and ends dangling from the frame.

He straightened and glanced at Jessica, who stood silently watching the chaos. The humidity of the hot afternoon had plastered her hair to her cheeks and neck. She swiped strands away from her eyes and heard him say in a dry tone, "I sure hope you don't teach driver's ed up there in Austin."

"Of course not," she snapped. Then she glanced around sheepishly to see who was listening to the conversation.

"Well." Jason's gaze switched back to the truck, "I hope you have good insurance." He glanced at her again. "You have insurance, don't you?"

"Certainly, I have insurance." Her secretary took care of such things, but Celeste was competent. "Yes. I—I think I do," she amended, feeling as though she was fifteen and in love with the guy again.

He gave her a tolerant look. "When do you think you might know—for sure? I drove this off the dealer's lot two hours ago."

"You just bought it?" Her heart sank. Drawing a deep breath, she started over. "What I mean is, I'm sure I do on my other car. I'll call my agent as soon as I get home and check. She'd fluffed off the insurance offer at the car rental. "I assure you, Jason, your truck will be taken care of," she said in her school-teacher-chastis-ing-a-naughty-child voice. *He must think I'm an idiot!* "Look, I'm really sorry about this. It's that darn gas pedal on Fred's truck. It keeps sticking on me." Heat burned in her cheeks. "I certainly didn't single your truck out, you know. I made every effort to avoid hitting it—and I could have been hurt, you know," she accused, feeling as wrong as gravy on potato salad.

Jason turned his direct, clear gaze back to roam her appearance. "Were you?"

"Was I what?" she shot back, slightly unnerved by his bold appraisal.

"Were you hurt?"

She gave an exasperated sigh. "Do I look like I'm hurt?"

A tiny, infuriating grin appeared as he observed. "No, little Jessie, your fine as a pretty patch of sunflowers."

There it was, that "little Jessie" bit.

"Look," he said brusquely, "I haven't got all day to haggle. I'm late for an appointment right now."

Jessica's knees turned to rubber now that his gaze had left her. She eyed his truck and decided the damage was great. She turned back to address him.

"What will you do? You can't drive it like that, can you?"

He frowned. "I doubt it. It doesn't look drivable."

"Want me to call a tow truck?"

A fella called from the storefront. "I'd make that the junk yard. That's where it's headed." Male laughter filled the air.

Heat flooded her cheeks again. "Looks like Fred's old bumper is only dented. Can I..." She swallowed against a dry throat. "Drop you somewhere?"

"If you're going my way. I was due at the bank ten

minutes ago. When I'm through, I'll have one of my men pick me up. Jim, can you call a wrecker?"

"Sure thing."

Jason reached up to remove the large Stetson and wipe sweat from his brow.

Jessica's heart caught in her throat as her eyes involuntarily drank in the mass of thick, golden-brown hair, which by now was nearly blond from endless hours in the hot Texas sun. Her eyes traveled slowly down the cut of the blue western shirt that was moistly molded to his broad, thick chest and the tight-fitting jeans, which made Jessica only too aware of an older, leaner, harder man than the one she had loved so fiercely eight years ago. The familiar weak longing crept over her as she forced her attention back to his words. She blushed hotly as she encountered a pair of lazy green eyes mockingly aware of her less-than-benign assessment of him.

He opened the door and stepped into the passenger side. Awkward moments passed until Jessica cleared her throat. "Sorry about your truck." Other than a tire rubbing the front fender Fred's truck was hardly touched.

"Material things. No one was hurt. There's four more like it sitting at the dealer."

That was Jason. Unusually calm. Competent. Independent. You would think he'd be a little rattled seeing her after all these years.

The stipulation of her aunt and uncle's will rang like a bell in her mind. Before she could second-guess herself, a question popped out.

"Would it be possible for you to stop by the house tonight?" Jessica bit her tongue to overcome the humiliation that swamped her. Did she seriously intend to discuss the will's stipulation? Well...maybe. It would be in a question form only. No commitments, just a question.

Surprise colored his features. "Come by your house

tonight? Why?"

The temperature must have risen ten degrees in the cab. Perspiration trickled down her back. "A small matter came up that I need to discuss with you, if you could spare a few minutes." This was bad. He was staring at her as if she had just escaped the looney bin.

"Is this something we could settle now?"

Jessica shot back. "I would need more than fifteen seconds to say what I have to say."

He shrugged. "I'll be by around seven."

Indecision nagged her. She was tired of eating dinner alone. There was no law that stated she couldn't have dinner with an old acquaintance. If he agreed to this crazy notion of helping her for the next six months—and that was a big *if*—then likely there would be plenty of cold sandwiches and hot coffee in their immediate future. Clearing her throat lightly, she added, "Marcy is welcome to come with you."

"Marcy Evans?"

"Is there another Marcy in town?"

He turned with a blank expression. "Why would Marcy Evans be coming with me?"

"Aunt Rainey said that you two were an item."

"Really. Huh." He shook his head. We hang out every once in a while, go to a movie, eat dinner but there's nothing territorial between me and Marcy." He adjusted the brim of his hat. "Is that what folks think? Me and Marcy?"

"According to Aunt Rainey—but we haven't talked about you in years." That was a bit of a stretch but close to the truth.

"I'll bring Sweet Thing." When he didn't add to the information, she let the subject drop, hoping he hadn't detected that brief—but no doubt evident—dip of her forehead. At least dreadful Marcy was out of the immediate picture.

He turned to grin at her, his strong white teeth

flashing in his bronze face. "Want me to bring dinner? I can stop by the café and have Melba make a couple of meatloaf sandwiches."

Sweet Thing must be the type that didn't eat.

Briefly closing her eyes, she imagined the scrumptious sandwich, meatloaf with green peppers and onions stuffed between two pieces of homemade white bread. Over the years she had often thought of ordering a dozen sandwiches and have Melba FEDEX them to her in Austin, but they wouldn't taste the same. Nothing did these days.

"I would love that."

"You supply the tea."

"Deal." The old truck rattled along, the tire scraping against the fender well. She imagined his thoughts. His new truck compared to this one. Right now, his new one wasn't in much better shape than this one.

"By the way, Marcy Evans married Willis Mercy last week."

"Marcy Evans married Bo Bo Mercy?" Jessica burst into laughter. "You're not serious! He's as dull as a brown shoe!"

"It's true. Bought a crockpot, and attended the ceremony myself."

She snickered. "Marcy Mercy. Serves her right."

"I'm sure your pastor would be pleased with you right about now."

She sobered. "I'm sorry, that was an unkind remark, it's just that—"

"You and Marcy liked to compete."

"Actually, I liked her and she liked me until our junior year..." She caught back her words. They'd been BBFs until they fell in love with the same boy. She gripped the steering wheel, tears of laughter running down her cheeks at the picture of the elegant Marcy Evans being married to Willis Mercy. "Marcy Mercy!"

Jason's cool reserve finally broke and he joined in

the laughter, both in near hysteria. She swerved the steering wheel, ran up on the curb and then swiftly got the truck back on pavement. A hubcap flew off and hit a street sign.

Somehow the near accident made the incident even funnier.

Jason finally managed to regain his composure and wiped his eyes on the arm of his blue shirt. His features wore a more tender expression as Jessica's laughter subsided. Soft violet eyes came slowly up to meet lazy green ones and he said in a gentle tone, "If you're asking me if I'm married, the answer is no. Not even close."

The bank came into view and she pulled the truck to the curb. Her gaze met his. "Well, you haven't asked, but I'm not married, either."

"I know."

Her gaze widened.

He winked. "Rainey and Fred have kept me well informed of your activities over the years. You have a successful clothing line, you drive a Jag and you came close to marrying a couple years back."

"Seems Rainey talked too much."

He laughed and got out of the truck. "See you around seven." He strode off in the direction of the bank.

"Sure, see you at seven." Her eyes followed his strong, manly form down the street. "And at eight, and nine, and in all my dreams for as long as I continue to remember."

Four

The old truck sped home smoothly, as if in sincere repentance for its bad behavior of the afternoon.

Jessica made a hurried change into cooler shorts and tank top, then flopped onto the Early American sofa to call Celeste.

"Hey, boss-lady," came her cheerful voice.

Jessica ignored the nickname, which her team knew irritated her, and plowed into the reason for the call. "Please tell me I have insurance."

"Sure. Health insurance. Life insurance. Home owner's—"

"Automobile insurance," she interjected. "Specifically, while driving a vehicle that belongs to someone else."

"Uh, hold on a sec." Fingers tapped on a keyboard at an astounding rate. "Indemnity, collision, blah, blah. Here it is. Yes, you're covered, after a five-hundred-dollar deductible." Curiosity entered her voice. "Who's car did you wreck?"

"My uncle's," she said. No reason in going into the whole embarrassing mess.

She jotted down the information she needed, including the policy number and the phone number for claims.

"Thanks, Celeste. Everything going okay there?"

"The place is running like a top. But we miss you. When are you coming home?"

Jessica's grip on the phone tightened. "As soon as I possibly can. I have a few things to settle here, but hopefully it won't take more than a few days."

When she'd disconnected the call, she flew around straightening the living room. It was a comfortable room with a sofa and chair placed before the large window. The sunlight streaming through cradled the green plants Aunt Rainey had hung. Dust lay thick on the maple end tables, and the air filled with the scent of lemons as Jessica applied furniture polish and rubbed until the wood gleamed. A large bouquet of flowers, fresh from the yard, rested in the center of the round glass coffee table in front of the sofa.

She moved to the kitchen and fed Tabby his dinner. The cat hovered around her legs, no doubt feeling lost without Rainey. Jessica knew how she felt. Being in this house where everything reminded her of Rainey left a residue of melancholy in Jessica's heart that no amount of busywork could banish. Could she force herself to give this place up? Hand it over to the church?

Surely Rainey and Fred would be proud of her---or maybe she could work something out with Jason to get past that stipulation in the will.

When the house looked as neat as if Raney had cleaned it herself, Jessica decided to have a quick shower and shampoo her hair before Jason arrived.

"I'm being ridiculous," she told Tabby. "You'd think I actually had a date with the man." Tabby sat with his tail curved around his feet, staring up at her. "I don't. This is just a business meeting, nothing personal. The subject of our past won't even come up. I simply have a disagreeable chore to do"

If he'd agree to help her with legal matters until she could receive her inheritance, then they could say goodbye forever.

Tabby began to groom his paw, appearing rather bored by the whole conversation. Jessica left him to it and climbed the stairs to the bathroom off the hall from her bedroom. She had her tank top halfway off when it occurred to her that she was out of shampoo. Drat! She'd intended to get some while she was out, but it had slipped her mind in in all the confusion of the day. A quick glance at her watch showed that she nearly an hour before Jason was due. Plenty of time to tootle down to the drugstore and back.

"Surely not one more thing could go wrong today." She grabbed her purse and keys, calling to Tabby on the way downstairs. "Hold the fort, I'll be right back."

Texas heat was terrible. The old seat in the truck was so hot on the backs of her legs she was forced to do a crazy dance trying to get the key turned on. The motor sprang to life.

"Good boy," Jessica told the truck as she gave the dash board an affectionate pate. Lavish praise for the cantankerous vehicle might sound stupid, but it couldn't hurt.

An empty parking space directly in front of the drugstore awaited her. Life was finally going her way.

Springing onto the hot sticky pavement, she hurried to push open the glass door of the drugstore. The smell of medicinal jars and bottles tickled her nose while cool air washed over her.

She found the shampoo display immediately, and studied the assorted bottles before her. No sign of the expensive product she used at home. A multitude of TV shampoo commercials flooded her mind. Biting her lip pensively, she struggled with the age-old problem. Did she want her hair shiny, swinging, voluptuous, full, or just plain clean? The image of a tall good-looking cowboy skipped lightly through her mind. Her hand hovered for a moment over the 'voluptuous' brand. Then she scolded herself. *This is a business meeting. Not a date.* She snatched the up 'squeaky clean' bottle and paid for the purchase.

She hopped back into the truck and turned the key. Nothing. The old gray relic just sat there, silent as a flat rock. "No! Don't do this to me." She jiggled the key. Nothing. "If you don't start, I'll...I'll kick your sorry rear bumper."

Apparently the truck did not respond to threats. Moaning, Jessica buried her hot, flushed face in her hands. This was turning out to be the longest day of her life. Now what was she going to do? Jason would be waiting when she got home. He couldn't see her looking like this. Dirty hair. Sweaty clothes.

Jerking the door handle, she slid out of the truck, marched around to the hood, yanked it open and stood staring helplessly into the yawning chasm of wires, gadgets and doodads. Everything in the engine looked like it needed to be replaced. Though she had many talents, she couldn't claim 'mechanic' as one of them. What was that wire there? She jiggled it a bit. Then found another one to jiggle. Praying silently for a miracle, she hopped back into the driver's seat and turned the ignition switch again.

Silence from the old truck.

Her temper registering a .9 on the Richter scale, she

stormed out of the truck. Her eyes glimpsed a large wrench lying in rusty bed of the vehicle. She snatched it and stomped to the hood again, defiance in every step. If the darned thing wouldn't cooperate, she'd bang its innards until it learned obedience. Over and over she brought the heavy wrench down. She leaned over into the motor, halfway burying herself in the engine, whacking at the contents without mercy.

The cashier from the drug store exited through the glass door and stood gaping at her.

Sweat rolled down Jessica's back, and her anger flared to a dangerous level. With a final vigorous whack to at battery, she straightened to survey the scene. All her work with the wrench didn't show a single dent. Disgusted, she wiped greasy hands on the back of her shorts and she climbed into the driver's seat.

"I've had it with you," she warned the vehicle.

A bead of sweat rolled off her nose. Nice.

This time when she turned the key, and the old engine purred sweetly to life. Jessica closed her eyes and slumped over the steering wheel. This truck was going to be the death of her.

She got back out one final time to slam down the old hood, which took three tries, before the lock caught. When she shoved the gearshift into first, a loud grounding noise filled the cab. A man passing on the sidewalk at that moment winced at the grating, tearing sound. A glance at her watch revealed she only had a few minutes before Jason arrived, and she still had to take a shower. Exhaustion tugged at her limbs. She felt as though she had worked on a chain gang this afternoon.

The last stoplight caught her at the end of town. She sat tapping her nails on the steering wheel, waiting for the green light. When the signal changed, she peeled out and flew along the unpaved road leading to the farmhouse. The last thing she needed today was a speeding ticket. She eased up on the gas pedal. Naturally, the truck refused to obey, but continued at the same speed. This truck was stepping on her last nerve.

As the driveway to Aunt Rainey's came into view, Jessica stomped the gas pedal, trying to un-stick it. Her left foot slammed on the brake hard, at the same time trying to negotiate the turn into the drive. The ancient speedometer registered twenty-eight. She was taking the turn at twenty-eight miles an hour! Aunt Rainey's few remaining chickens set up a terrible squawking, feathers flying as they scrambled to safety.

Jessica shot into the farmyard at the speed of a bullet, her eyes widening in astonishment when she spotted a gray Lincoln Continental in the driveway. What was that doing there? The thought barely had time to register before the truck came to a grinding halt—its front bumper embedded in the Continental's rear end.

She closed her eyes as the melodious tinkle of the lenses falling from the Lincoln's taillights broke the silence. Her heart sank as the old engine died a sputtering death.

The tall man standing on the porch, about to knock on the door, spun around at the sound of the crash. Jason. Her spirits sank to her flip-flops. A look of sheer incredulity crossed his features as he walked slowly down the steps, toward Jessica's side of the truck. He glanced at the back of his car with a stunned expression and then turned to face her.

In a very small, defensive voice, she said, "You're early."

Still not taking his eyes from her, he leaned casually against the remains of his bumper and stared at her.

Her breath caught in her chest, Jessica was afraid to move.

He exhaled a slow breath and spoke in a calm voice. "Did you check on your insurance?"

She nodded, and managed to squeak out, "I have

good insurance."

"It had better be *darn* good."

She released her breath in a quick spurt. "It's the gas pedal again!"

Jason shoved away from the truck, his jaw clenching and unclenching. Was he holding back anger? Not that she could blame him if he were. A moment later she was sure of it, when he jerked her door open with so much force she wouldn't have been surprised if it had broken the hinges.

Heat that had nothing to do with the Texas sun filled her face. Even the tips of her ears burned. This day had been chock-full of emotion, not a single one good. It was too much. To her horror, tears stung her eyes, and no amount of blinking could hold them back. She was going to cry, right here in front of the one person she didn't want to display any emotions to. Her shoulders began to shake, and she buried her face in her hands and bawled like a baby.

"Oh, *shoot.*"

A set of strong arms wrapped around her and lifted her out of the truck. She was held against a firm, solid chest. The clean fragrance of soap and aftershave swirled about her. She sobbed even harder.

"Come on now, Angel." He stroked the hot, sticky hair away from her forehead. "No need to cry over a car." He cleared his throat. "Or two."

The sound of his old nickname, the name she never thought to hear again, opened a new floodgate.

"I—I'm so sorry." She wiped her eyes on his shoulder, and then struggled out of his hold. He set her down, but when her flip-flops were firmly on the ground, didn't move away. Hot, salty tears continued to run in streams down her face.

"Hey, it's not that bad." He placed a knuckle under her chin and lifted her face to his. "The insurance will take care of it."

"I know, but it's not just the wrecked vehicles." The words shuddered out of her heaving chest. "You can't begin to *imagine* what a nightmare this day has been."

With a gentle gesture, he smoothed her hair back from her face and tucked it around her ear. "I think I can. Mine hasn't been what you'd call a red-letter day either." His eyes took in his wrecked car.

With an attempt, she choked back the worst of the tears. He must think her a complete ninny. "I'm so sorry about your truck—and now your car. Then there's that ridiculous will." She sniffled loudly. "And then this—this—despicable piece of junk." Her foot shot out to level a firm kick on the truck. "It has done nothing but torment me all day."

"Well, it could be worse," he said with not much conviction. "I don't think the car has quite as much damage as the truck."

"Really?" Her spirits lifted slightly.

He rubbed his thumb across her cheek. "You're covered in oil or something."

The hint of amusement in his eyes more than his comment did much to dispel the last of the tears. What would her employees think if they could see their 'boss-lady' in such a state? She was usually more composed than this.

"I—I need to clean up. Shall we go inside?"

He gestured for her to precede him to the house. On the porch, he stooped to retrieve a white paper bag he'd dropped there—their sandwiches, probably—and followed her through the door.

When he stepped into the living room, he pitched his Stetson in Uncle Fred's big reclining chair in front of the stone fireplace, a habit so familiar she caught her breath. Some things never changed, like the way the enduring habit tugged at her heart strings. Ties she thought were long broken.

"Would you like some iced tea while I clean up?"

Jessica asked, already on her way to the kitchen.

He followed her. "Sounds good to me. Plenty of ice." Sliding into a seat at the oak table, his gaze roamed around the room. "Boy, does this kitchen bring back memories."

Though she'd give all she owned to know his thoughts, she bit back the question. Were they happy memories? Bad ones? Regrettable ones?

"I'd like to have a nickel for every piece of Rainey's apple pie I've eaten in here." He laughed.

A smile tugged at Jessica's lips as she removed a tray of ice from the freezer compartment of the refrigerator. "You'd be a wealthy man," she joked.

Tabby sauntered into the room as she set a tall glass of tea—with plenty of ice—in front of him. The cat sat primly beside Jason's chair, looking up at him with an unmistakable request in his feline eyes.

"Oh, okay, pest." Jason obliged, and reached down to stroke the cat, who arched into his hand.

Jessica snatched up the bag from the drug store. "I'll leave you to entertain each other. I'll only be a few minutes." She hurried from the room without waiting for an answer. Having him here, in this house where they'd spent so many hours as teenagers in love, played on her nerves more than she'd anticipated.

On the way to the bathroom she snatched a clean pair of shorts and a tee-shirt from her suitcase. She locked the bathroom door, and then tested the handle with a jiggle. Not that Jason would try anything. Even as a teenager he'd treated her with respect in that regard, though at times resisting the physical urges had been almost more than either of them could withstand. Even after their failed marriage, when loving each other would have been perfectly legal—for the few days it lasted—they had remained chaste, for which Jessica had been thankful many times over the years.

Showers were necessarily short in this house, but

tonight Jessica broke records. When she'd dried off, donned fresh clothes, and brushed her hair, she stood in front of the mirror. Wiping a clear circle from the steamy glass, she inspected herself. Wet locks of hair the color of Texas wheat fell midway-down her back. When the humidity finished its job, it would look three times as thick as it already was. Should she blow it dry? She decided not to, nor did she opt for applying makeup. This was a business meeting, nothing else. Instead, she fished in the vanity drawer until she found a scrunchee, and pulled the wet tresses into a pony tail at the back of her neck.

She returned to the kitchen rubbing lotion into her hands, and found him refilling his tea glass.

"I helped myself," he said with a hint of apology, which she waved off.

"Pour one for me too, would you?"

She picked up the paper bag and carried it to the counter.

"Wait." She turned to him. "What happened to your date?"

A blank look settled on his features. "My date?"

"Sweet Thing. Couldn't she make it?"

A chuckle rumbled from deep in his chest. "She's here. Outside."

"Out—" Realization hit Jessica, and she shut her eyes in renewed mortification. "Sweet Thing's your car, isn't she?" At his nod, she moaned. "Not so sweet-looking at the moment."

He shrugged. "That's what insurance is for."

The only reason a man would name a car is if he really enjoyed owning it. She'd destroyed not only his brand-new pickup, but his favorite car as well. Humiliation burned in her cheeks.

"Hey." He spoke softly. "It's okay. Really. We'll let the insurance companies handle things."

With a grateful smile, she took down two dinner

plates from the cabinet. Their elbows touched when he reached for a second tea glass, and something like an electric shock zipped up Jessica's arm. She hurried back to the table. Being back in this place, with all those memories so fresh and tender, was messing with her emotions. Their relationship had ended a long time ago. Best keep it that way.

Jason returned to the table as Jessica unwrapped the sandwiches and set one on each plate.

"I'm afraid I was neglectful in my visits to Rainey and Fred in the last few years," he admitted.

Jessica set a plate in front of his chair. "I know what you mean. Especially after Fred passed on, I should have spent more time here, with Rainey. And now it's too late."

"I'm sure it's hard to find time to get away from your company." He placed her tea glass in front of her, and slid the sugar bowl within reach. She hid a smile. Funny how he remembered that she liked her tea sweet, while she remembered that he didn't.

They seated themselves on opposite sides of the small table. Out of a decades-old habit, they sat facing each other across the table from the sides, leaving the chairs at the head and foot of the table—Fred's and Rainey's—empty.

He picked up half of his sandwich and, with his elbows planted on either side of his plate, held it before his mouth. "So, tell me, Jessie. How's life treated you over the years?"

"Very well. And you?" Rainey had kept her informed of his activities. He'd gone from a small farmer to one of the largest land holders in the area. He had yet to marry, though according to Rainey he could have his pick of fillies in the area. According to Rainey, he favored women with brains more than silicone.

"You're prettier than ever," he added in a light tone.

Her cheeks heated. "Thank you." She started to return the compliment, but changed her mind. This conversation needed to steer clear of personal stuff."

He raised his glass. "Rainey said you're quite a success. Ladies jeans?"

"That's right. The line is called Fancy Duds. My partner and I started the business a few years back."

"They sell well?"

"Better than I ever dreamed they would. Yes, I would say the business is successful."

She bit into the sandwich and closed her eyes to enjoy the taste that brought back a million memories. If her taste buds could do back-flips, they would. She chewed with relish.

"Businesses can be a big headache," Jason commented before taking a bite of his own sandwich.

"I hear you're doing okay." She hesitated, and then related what Rainey had told her. "Seems you own about everything around here, don't you?"

"Not everything, but I have my fair share." He flashed a grin and gulped his tea. "I would have thought you'd be married again by now, with a couple of kids, white picket fence and county socials every Saturday night."

She offered a short ironic laugh. "Afraid not. Running the business keeps me too busy."

Time for this conversation to take another turn. She set her sandwich down, her stomach queasy from a sudden attack of nerves. "Speaking of business, I invited you over tonight to discuss a business matter."

He picked up his glass of tea again. "What did you want to see me about, Jessica?"

For some reason, she had trouble thinking clearly while looking into those intense green eyes. She stood and walked over to the large kitchen window to gaze for a moment at Aunt Rainey's sweet-smelling lily patch, trying to bolster her courage. Drawing a deep breath, she turned back to face him.

"Uncle Fred and Aunt Rainey's will surprised me."

He cocked his head, curiosity apparent. "How so? You're the only heir, aren't you?"

"Yes," she answered quickly. "Well, sort of."

"Sort of?"

She bit down on her lower lip. This was harder than she'd expected. *Spit it out, Jessica.*

Turning to face him, she clutched the edge of the counter behind her back and blurted out the awful truth.

"Jason, I need you."

Five

Surprise flashed onto his face, while heat rose into Jessica's. Probably not the best way to introduce the matter.

"Uh, let me explain."

Eyebrows arched up beneath his hair, he gave a nod. "That would be good."

She drew in a breath. "In order for me to inherit Fred and Rainey's estate, I have to return home and run this farm for six months. Either that, or it will go to Manor Methodist Church." She rushed on. "Not that I have anything against the church inheriting. Fred and Rainey loved that church. But I can't let them have it. The farm is mine, which means I'll have to run it for six months."

The muscles in Jason's forearm tensed before he

drained his glass. "How do you propose to do that? Do you know anything about running a farm?" He set his empty glass back down on the table.

"Absolutely nothing. I've been gone so many years I wouldn't have the slightest idea what to do with all those cows standing out there." She waved a hand in the general direction of the pasture behind the house.

Jason left the table to go to the refrigerator for more tea. "You were raised here. You'd do better than you think."

"I don't want to come back here and run this farm." Her grip on the counter tightened. "It burns me to think that Uncle Fred and Aunt Rainey, even in death, have managed to tear my life up once again—" She stopped mid-sentence, yet another flush rising into her face.

Jason filled his glass, replaced the pitcher, and then stood with his back against the refrigerator. "Then don't do it. Your business is doing well, you said so yourself. You don't need the money."

His unemotional attitude helped to steady her. "That's true. But I have an expansion goal that I think could make a huge difference in my company. I want to open a line of designer children's clothing." She drew a steadying breath. "I can't endanger the company's financial status by making the initial investment, but with the money I'd get from selling this farm in six months..." She shrugged. The dream of the new clothing line had been just that—a dream—until Rainey's death. Not that she would wish her aunt ill for anything in the world, but suddenly that dream was within reach...almost. Frustrated, she clenched her hand into a fist and smacked the countertop. "I can't for the life of me imagine why they wouldn't let me make my own decisions. My gosh, I'm twenty-five years old now—perfectly able to take care of myself."

"Perfectly." Jason accompanied the sarcastic comment with a pointed glance through the window, where his Lincoln sat in the driveway.

Jessica's gaze followed his. "Jason, I said I was sorry. Believe me, I've always had a perfect driving record."

"Well, you blew that today, didn't you?"

As she was about to launch a verbal dart in return, he lifted a hand. "I'm sorry. That was uncalled-for." He retrieved his empty plate from the table and carried it to the sink. "I assume you asked me here for more than a meatloaf sandwich. What do you need from me?"

A dreadful flutter erupted in her stomach. Now that the time had come, could she force herself to ask him? "You don't have any trouble running your big ranch, do you?"

Jason's features took on a guarded expression, his eyes narrowing. "No. Why?"

Asking for a personal favor wouldn't be appropriate. But what about appealing to his business side? "You're a business man, and I'm offering you a business opportunity." She turned a bright smile on him. "Would you run the farm for me?"

Jason's mouth dropped open. Jessica's heart thudded as she plunged on. "Don't answer yet. I know what you're thinking, because at first, I thought the same thing. We didn't exactly part friends eight years ago, but now we're two mature adults. I'm willing to set aside our old differences—"

"Just hold it right there," Jason said between clenched teeth.

"No, please, hear me out." Though his features remained blank, his body language spoke volumes. Strong arms were folded tightly across his chest. He leaned back against the refrigerator as if he wished he could put even more distance between them. Somehow, she had to convince him to run this farm for her. She raised her chin. "I'll pay you thirty thousand dollars."

His eyebrows arched.

"Just think, Jason, thirty thousand dollars. You could buy some new farm equipment, a new car." She cast a guilty glance out the window. "Okay, maybe not a car, because my insurance is going to make that one good as new, and your truck too. But surely thirty thousand dollars could come in handy for something. You could just consider it your mad money."

He interrupted her again. "Look, Jessie, the last thing in the world I need is your mon—"

"Jason, please!" She folded her hands together and placed them under her chin in a clear posture of begging. "I don't know anyone else to ask."

He stared at her for a long time, before finally unfolding his arms. Then he began to pace between the fridge and the window. "Let me get this straight. You want me to run this farm for the next six months...why? As a favor to an old friend?"

"For thirty thousand dollars," Jessica hurried to insert.

Jason dismissed the comment with an impatient flip of his hand. "I'm supposed to become your hired hand, to hop over here every day, run your farm, and forget all about what happened eight years ago" He shook his head slowly. "Do you know what you're asking?"

Was the sight of her so repugnant to him, then? The idea smarted.

"You wouldn't have to see me much," Jessica promised resentfully. "I'd stay out of your way."

"That isn't the point." He came to a halt in front of her, his eyes like green ice. "There's not enough money in the world to make me put myself back in that emotional blender you had me in years ago. I've spent eight long years trying to get you out of my blood. I'm not about to let you do that to me again."

A tense muscle worked along his jaw. With a shock, the sight brought back a flood of memories. That muscle ticked whenever emotions threatened to overpower Jason. Did he still hate her so much, then?

"I had no choice," she whispered softly. "Surely you know that."

"You had choices."

He stood so close she felt the heat of his breath on her face. Her bones threatened to turn to jelly, and she braced herself against the counter.

"Did I? What choice did I really have? I was under age, and Uncle Fred had a serious heart condition. Plus, I owed them a tremendous debt of gratitude for taking me into their home, for loving me as their own child. I couldn't break their hearts."

"So instead you broke mine," Jason said.

"And mine, too." Her voice was a mere whisper.

She shut her eyes against the resurgence of the agony she'd felt that day, eight years ago, when she said goodbye to her happily-ever-after out of duty.

"It doesn't matter, Jessie." She opened her eyes to see him step back from her. "You'll never have the opportunity to do it again."

Jessica felt the sun had gone behind a cloud as the warmth of his body moved away from her.

In the next instant, her temper rapidly boiled to the surface. She stomped across the floor to confront him. "Well, if you were so all-fired brokenhearted over me, why didn't you come after me—fight harder for me—do something other than just walk away? I never even saw you again until the other day at the cemetery, Jason Rawlings."

"You made your choice that morning, right here in this room, Ms. Cole." He stabbed a finger at the floor where she stood.

Her hands clenched into fists, and she fought to keep them at her side instead of pounding him. "If you had loved me, that wouldn't have stopped you."

"If you had loved me, there would have been no

choice," Jason shot back.

With an effort, she forced herself to calm, though could not manage to unclench her hands. "I don't know how we got into this discussion in the first place." Her voice filled the tiny kitchen, and she lowered her voice. "Will you or will you not run this farm for me for the next six months?"

"I'll think about it." Jason shot back, then stomped from the room.

She was unable to filter the sarcasm from her tone. "Well, by all means, let me know when you reach a decision."

He snatched his hat off Uncle Fred's chair, gave her one last disgusted look, and slammed out of the farmhouse. She raced to the window to watch his retreat. When he reached his car, he shot another dirty look at the window, backed out of the drive, and, with his back bumper dragging on the ground, sped away.

Jessica had just stepped out of a hot bath an hour later when her cell rang. Wrapping herself in an oversized fleecy towel, she ran to answer it.

"Hello."

"I'll run your farm for you."

Though she had to pull the phone from her ear at the volume of Jason's gruff shout, relief washed over her in a wave that left her weak-kneed.

Her reply waited a moment until she could ensure a polite tone. "Thank you."

"I'll be by in the morning to discuss the details. All right?"

"All right."

The call ended abruptly from his end. She kissed her cell phone and did a happy little hop down the hall.

"I'll be here," she told Tabby, her exuberance echoing off the walls.

Tabby opened one disinterested eye. Apparently, he couldn't care less.

Six

A loud, insistent knocking on the front door brought Jessica out of a sound sleep early the next morning. Fumbling for her robe, she groped her way downstairs, her head still fuzzy from sleep.

"I'm coming. I'm coming," she shouted.

When she arrived, she jerked the door open to find a grinning Jason on the porch. Leaning wearily against the doorsill, she glared purple daggers. "Do you realize what time it is?"

"Yep. It's gettin' late." He made a point of examining his watch. "Almost six o'clock."

This was an uncivilized community. She sagged more heavily against the door. "I didn't hear you drive up."

One golden brown brow arched high. "I haven't got

anything to drive up in. I rode my horse over. I told her "good luck—you're going to need it."

Jessica caught sight of the roan mare tearing up mouthfuls of grass behind him.

"Surely," he continued brightly, "you haven't forgotten how early a farmer's day begins."

"I've tried my best to." She attempted a smile, which probably looked a bit sheepish. She rarely made her way out of Starbucks with a skinny vanilla latte by nine o'clock.

"Well, Angel," he said matter-of-factly, "you'd better refresh your memory. We've got a lot of things to talk over."

Placing a hand on each of her upper arms, he turned her in the direction of the kitchen.

"Coffee would be good." He gave her a slight push.

She stumbled forward, aware that he fell in step behind her, chuckling. Was he always in such a good mood this early in the morning? She filled the coffeepot with water. Setting it back down on the counter, she stood on tiptoe to reach the can of coffee on the top shelf.

"Allow me." He plucked the coffee can off the high shelf and presented it to her like it was a gift of diamonds being given to a queen. Their fingers touched, and a thrill surged up her arm. She snatched the can and stepped back.

"Thanks," she managed to grind out.

He slid into a chair at the table and watched as she spooned grounds into the basket. As she plugged in the pot to perk she asked grudgingly, "Have you had breakfast?" If he was going to work for her, she might as well try to get along with him.

"Two hours ago."

"Oh goodness." Jessica slid into the chair opposite him. "All right, then, where do we start?"

"First of all, I need to hire at least three men to help

run this farm."

Jessica yawned, planted an elbow on the table and rested her chin in the palm of her hand. "Fine with me." Her eyes drifted shut. She could sure use another hour or two of sleep.

"Second—Jessica, look at me when I'm talking."

She pried open bleary eyes.

Shaking his head, he continued. "Second, I don't have room for three more men on my farm, so they will have to stay here."

Jessica raised her head. "Here?"

"That's right. In fact, if you have no objections, I'm going to move three of my own men in, too. My bunkhouse is too crowded as it is now."

As the meaning of his request became clear, she came fully awake. "You want me to live in this house with six strange men?"

Jason laughed. "That would sure give the folks in town a reason to wag their tongues. No, you'll be coming over to live at my house. Next, how much working capital do you have on hand? There's some fence down in several areas—"

"Wait a minute." Jessica shook her head with a jerk, trying to grasp everything. "Let's back up to the part where I live at your house."

A bland expression overtook his features. "What about it?"

"Humor me, please, and elaborate on that just a hair more." She smiled with saccharine sweetness.

"Certainly. My housekeeper's sister had major surgery and will need constant care for a while. Mrs. Perkins left last week and won't be back for several months at least." He stood, and crossed the floor to the coffeepot. "Now, if I have to run two farms, I won't have time to find a new housekeeper. So, in essence, Jessica, if I'm going to do you a favor, you'll do one for me in return."

"But, I'm *paying* you to run this farm." She didn't bother to filter the heat from her tone.

He shrugged. "All right. I'll pay you to run my house."

Jessica ran fingers through her sleep-tangled hair. What a mess. She understood his reasoning, but she didn't like it, not one bit. How could Uncle Fred and Aunt Rainey have done this to her?

"I don't like it." She got up to pour herself a cup of coffee, since Jason had filled only his own.

"Take it or leave it." Jason sipped from his mug.

"Would you still run the farm if I refused?" she asked hopefully.

"No."

She glanced around the room, desperate to come up with an argument. Her gaze fell on the cat's food bowl. "Who will feed the cat?"

"I'm sure the men are capable of taking care of a cat."

"Talk about wagging tongues." She blew steam from the surface of her coffee and took a cautious sip. "If I agree to this they'll have a field day, given our, uh, history."

His lips twisted into the lopsided grin she used to love. "When have you ever cared about what the gossips say?"

She plucked an errant curl out of her eyes and tucked it behind her ear. What a predicament. Here she was, co-owner of a successful clothing company, about to become the maid for her ex-husband. But what choice did she have?

"I assume you have high-speed Internet," she said. "I'll still need to work. My company can't run itself. And I might have to fly to Austin for meetings every so often."

That might dissuade him. To her disappointment, he nodded. "That's understandable."

Just then the cat sauntered into the room and began twining himself around her legs. "Can I bring Tabby with me?"

Jason sighed. "If you insist."

Jessica slumped dejectedly back down into her chair. "I guess I'll do it."

"I thought you'd see things my way." Jason also returned to the table. "Get your things packed today, and I'll pick you up later this afternoon and take you over to the house."

She gasped. "So soon? Can't we wait a few days?"

"I have a business to run too," he told her sternly. "As soon as these living arrangements are settled, I can get on with my work."

Lifting the mug to her lips, she studied him over the rim. This was certainly a different Jason than had stormed out of here last night.

"I thought you didn't want me around, or to be involved with me in any way."

"I don't. But as you pointed out, we are reasonable adults, and this is too good a proposition to pass up. Thirty thousand dollars is a lot of 'mad money,' Angel."

That old nickname again. Disappointment stabbed at her. Nickname or not, his answer wasn't exactly flattering. Well, what had she expected? She had known all along if he agreed, it would be for the money.

He set his mug down and rested both arms on the table. Leaning toward her, he caught and held her gaze. "Let's get one thing clear right up front. This is a business arrangement only. Nothing personal."

Fire assaulted her cheeks. "Of course not."

"I mean it," he continued, his eyes still locked with hers. "Don't misunderstand the reason for these living arrangements. You'll be my housekeeper—nothing else."

What did he think, that she'd jump at the chance to resume their long-dead relationship? She lifted her nose high in the air. "I wouldn't have it any other way," she assured him.

"Fine. Just so we understand each other." His chair scraped across the linoleum as he stood and then took his coffee mug to the sink. "Will you be ready by five o'clock?"

She glanced around the room. There wasn't much to pack, really. This hadn't been her home for a long time. She nodded.

"Fine." He picked up his Stetson and placed it firmly on his head. "I'll see you then."

Without waiting for a reply, he strode from the room.

"I know it's a long time, Barb." Jessica cocked her head sideways and held her cell phone to her ear with a shoulder. "Trust me, I don't like this any more than you do."

She dumped the laundry basket onto the bed and picked up a blouse, still warm from the dryer.

"Are you sure there's not a loophole?" Her partner and co-owner of Fancy Duds came as close to a whine as she'd ever heard. "Maybe our attorney could take a look at that will and come up with something."

"I tried already," Jessica said. "I faxed him a copy yesterday."

"Nothing, huh?"

Jessica laid the folded blouse in her suitcase. "Judge Baker might be a small-town lawyer, but he's sharp as a tack. The will is iron-clad." She poured confidence into her voice. "You can handle anything that comes up. After all, you run half the company already."

"The boring half," Barb said bitterly. "What if we have a design problem, or something goes wrong in operations or marketing? I'll be lost."

Barb had always been the financial brain of their

partnership. Anything that had to do with numbers or computer systems fell under her area of control, and she kept those departments humming along. Jessica's talents lay in the opposite direction. Their clothing designs were all hers, and she loved all aspects of marketing and advertising.

"It's not like I'm moving to the wilds of Africa," Jessica said. "I'm as close as a phone call or an email. Just consider me a remote employee for a limited period of time."

A sigh blasted through the phone. "I guess I don't have a choice."

The last piece of laundry folded and placed in her suitcase, Jessica flopped onto the bed. "Trust me, if there were any other way, I'd be all over it. There isn't. On the other hand, when this ordeal is over we'll have the money we need for the children's clothing line."

"That's the silver lining," Barb admitted.

"You bet it is." Jessica glanced at the clock on the nightstand. "Listen, I've got to run. Celeste has my temporary address. I'm not sure if there's a fax machine, but if not I'll have one installed in the next few days."

"What do you mean you're not sure? Aren't you at your aunt and uncle's house?"

Jessica set her teeth. She didn't want to tell anyone, even her best friend and business partner, about her arrangement with Jason. It was too...humiliating.

"It's a long story." She prayed that Barb would let the matter drop.

She did.

"All right, girlfriend. You take it easy, and watch your step."

"What do you mean by that?"

"You're on a cattle farm, right? Just be careful not to step into anything icky."

Little did Barb know, but Jessica was hog wallowing in "icky".

Laughing, Jessica ended the call. She sat a minute longer, staring at the cell phone. Her laughter died when she realized Barb's warning had come too late. She was about to become her ex-husband's housekeeper. Was there anything ickier than that?

Seven

Jessica was packed and ready when one of Jason's men dropped him by the farm late that afternoon. After a quick glance at her packed bags Jason advised her, "We'll have to take your truck." Jessica shrugged her shoulders, unconcerned, and reached down for her cosmetic bag.

As they started down the porch steps Jason held out his hand. Jessica looked at it in bewilderment. "What do you want?"

"The keys to the truck." His voice was firm.

"Why? I can drive."

"Bet me," Jason said sarcastically.

She breathed out with a huff and flung the keys to him. Brother. He would never let her live those car wrecks down.

They drove back to his house in strained silence. Jessica's ride on the passenger side of the old truck was as nerve-racking as the rest of the cantankerous old relic. Her seat was loose at the bottom, so it swayed and made a popping noise every time Jason stopped for a stop sign or started up after one. A couple times she had to grab for something solid to keep from sliding out of the seat onto the floor.

And what was with all the stops, anyway? She could never recall having to stop so often. Jason seemed to be determined to make as many as possible. She caught him once watching her from the corner of his eye, not bothering to conceal a devilish twinkle.

At last they turned into the winding drive leading to his farmhouse. Sycamore trees towered over them from both sides, creating a shady canopy over the road. They traveled on for another mile or so before coming to the house itself—a lovely, homey, one-story brick home nestled in a stand of majestic old oak trees. The carpet of early-summer grass sparkled emerald green, and a riot of flowers bloomed around the yard. A large red barn with a tractor and several pieces of farm machinery sat just to the right of the house, with several gleaming white outbuildings in the distance. The white fences surrounding the farm all looked newly painted and well-tended.

Jason stopped the old truck and turned off the key. "I thought you said you were having trouble with the gas pedal sticking on this?"

"It does." She practically took his head off, but she had noticed, too, that the traitorous thing had purred along like a Cadillac with Jason at the wheel.

He cocked his head skeptically. "Remind me to take a look at it before you drive it again. I'd hate to turn you loose on the townspeople before it's fixed."

Jessica slid to the ground on her side of the truck

and slammed the door. "How many times do I have to say, I'm sorry?" She planted a hand on her hip and delivered a snarky barb. "What do you want—blood?"

He laughed. "You've lost your sense of humor over the years."

Jessica refused even to dignify the statement with an answer. Instead, she fell in step beside him toward a wide screened-in porch off the back entrance to the house. A golden retriever bounded toward them, made a friendly lunge at Jessica and nearly knocked her off her feet.

"Get down, Alfie," Jason scolded. "You better show some manners. This ill-tempered lady is going to be the new hand that feeds your face."

The dog ignored him and continued to lick Jessica's hands, his tail wagging so hard it was nearly throwing him off balance.

Jessica was returning pat for lick. "Don't believe a word this nasty man tells you, Alfie. I'll feed you, manners or not." Looking at Jason, she added sweetly, "After all, I'll have to feed your master, and he doesn't have any."

Apparently satisfied he still had a meal ticket, Alfie gave one last wag and loped back toward the barn.

Jessica picked up her cosmetic bag again and continued toward the house. A shrill whistle reached them. Turning, she located the source down by the barn. A nice-looking man, around her own age, waved a hand and began to stride swiftly toward them from the barnyard.

"Hey, Jason, wait up!"

"What is it, Rick?" Jason paused beside Jessica, his eyes narrowing slightly.

Eyeing Jessica appreciatively, Rick approached the couple. "Who's the pretty lady, boss?"

"Jessica Cole, meet Rick Warner. Jessica is my...new housekeeper."

"Housekeeper? Dang, what agency did you get her from? I'm going to give them a call. I think the bunk house needs a housekeeper." Rick grinned broadly.

Uncomfortable to be the object of Rick's appraising stare, Jessica managed a hesitant smile, but shifted slightly closer to Jason.

"Cool it, Rick." Jason's eyes flashed a silent warning. "Did you want something?"

"Yow. The garage called and said it would be a couple of weeks on your car and truck." He cocked his head. "How did you manage to tear both of them up all in the same day?"

A blush threatened as Jessica caught Jason's eye. *Please don't tell him!*

"Just lucky, I guess," he answered flippantly, and then turned toward the door.

"See you around, pretty lady." Rick tipped his hat, his tone optimistic.

"Glad to have met you," Jessica told him politely.

"Don't be taking up the men's time with a lot of idle chatter." Jason gave her a warning glare as they entered the house.

"Oh, I won't, Master. If you'll just throw some stale bread and water in the door occasionally, I promise no one will ever know I'm around." She stepped around him into the kitchen.

It had been many years since she had been in this room, but everything was still as she remembered. The rest of the house was much smaller, in general, than Uncle Fred and Aunt Rainey's, but Jessica had always loved this kitchen more than any other room in the whole house. It had a cozy, warm feeling with windows across one whole wall on the south, letting in all the light and sunshine anyone could desire. The round glass kitchen table sat in front of the windows, with a large sliding glass door leading out to a covered patio.

Cheery Cape Cod curtains hung at the windows, blending with the stainless-steel dishwasher, stove, and refrigerator. A long island bar ran almost the length of the kitchen, the marble counter tops and farmer's sink providing enough space for any woman to "create" to her heart's content.

They passed through the kitchen into the living room, and Jessica's heart fell as she saw the drab color scheme in here. She had always liked lots of color in her decorating, and although the furniture was of good quality, the tones were all drab browns and greens. Plain—that was the word she would use to describe it—just downright plain.

Jason noticed the change of expression on her face. "Mom always loved her kitchen best, so she never spent much time on the rest of the house."

Was that a touch of defensiveness in his tone?

He had been born and raised in this house with his brothers, Eric and Randall, and had stayed on here when his parents passed away several years ago. Eric had married and was living in Dallas with his wife and their small child, and Randall was working in the oil fields in Texas, never having married. That much Jason had told her on the way over, but little else. Trying to get anything personal out of him was like trying to pull hen's teeth. He didn't waste time on idle chitchat.

Jessica's gaze ran over the massive red brick fireplace that covered one whole wall on the north side, while wide, airy windows like those in the kitchen stretched across the south wall. The rays of the late-evening sun poured through them, falling on a monstrous plant that looked out of place sitting in the room. What was this, a jungle? The poor, sick plant appeared to have been through the ravages of war. The few leaves remaining on its limbs were limp and turning yellow. Just her gaze resting on it made it give up another leaf to the floor. And what was that peculiar odor? A step in that direction confirmed that the unpleasant smell came from the plant.

Jessica approached it hesitantly. Peering into its large clay pot, she saw a huge glob of coffee grounds lying on the soil.

"What's this?" she asked Jason suspiciously.

"My plant." He walked over to peer into the clay pot with her, deep concern written on his face. "It doesn't seem to be doing very well."

That had to be the understatement of the year.

"I don't understand what I'm doing wrong." He planted one hand on his slender hips and gestured toward the pathetic plant with the other. "I've tried everything people have suggested, but I can't seem to get it back on its feet."

She scrunched her nose. "What is that rotten, nauseous smell?"

"Oh, that? It's fish emulsion."

"Fish emulsion? What is that?"

"It's plant food. The girl at Wal-Mart said it was a good one." He gave a sniff, and then winced. "To be honest, the smell gets pretty rank in the heat of the day."

Jessica couldn't help it. A laugh bubbled out. "Maybe you should take it out on the patio and let the sun absorb the smell on the days you feed it the plant food."

Judging by the look that came over his face, you would have thought she had suggested they take a gun and shoot Alfie.

"Move that plant?" Troubled green eyes widened. "Why, there wouldn't be a leaf left on it."

"You certainly have a point there," she conceded.

"Believe it or not," he said, a bit defensively, "it's looking better than it did."

He started down the wide green-carpeted hall, calling over his shoulder, "This will be your bedroom."

Throwing open the first door on the left, he stepped

back and waited for her to enter. She sidled by, careful not to touch him, and entered a room roughly the size of her walk-in closet back in Austin.

"*This* is my bedroom?" She whirled to face him, astonished.

He shrugged. "This is the housekeeper's quarters."

"But—but—" She turned in a circle to eye the spartan furnishings. A single bed with no headboard or footboard took up most of the space. A tiny nightstand had been wedged between the bed and the side wall. Eighteen inches from the bottom of the mattress stood a closet with a curtain hung in place of a door. She pulled back the curtain to peek inside, and found the chest of drawers.

Swinging back toward him, Jessica put on her sternest expression. "This won't work at all. There's barely enough room to hang my dresses."

A sardonic twitch tugged the corners of his lips. "What do you need dresses for? It thought you made fancy jeans for a living."

She ignored the jab. "What about Eric's old room? Why can't I sleep there?"

He leaned against the doorsill. "It's full of horse tack."

With an effort, she suppressed an eye-roll. "Then how about Randall's? He doesn't live here anymore."

"Not permanently, but his stuff is all over the place in there. Working on an oil rig, he travels light."

Her mind followed the path of the hallway behind him, filling in the rooms from memory. The room next to Eric's used to belong to Jason, and their parents' bedroom lay at the end of the hall.

She gave him a suspicious look. "Where do you sleep?"

"The master, of course." A cocky grin spread across his tanned face. "Didn't you just call me Master?"

Her teeth ground in frustration. Should she ask to

sleep in his old bedroom? Distasteful as the idea was...she glanced around the tiny cell.

"Before you ask," he said, "my old room is off limits. I've stored a lot of Mom and Dad's stuff in there, and I don't want you messing with it."

She bristled at the implication that she would 'mess with' his parents' belongings.

"Fine," she snapped. "I'll stay in this room on one condition."

His eyebrows drew together. "What's that?"

"That you install a lock on this door."

He jumped out of the way in time to avoid being smacked with the door when she slammed it shut.

Eight

A noise in another part of the house drew Jessica from a deep sleep. She lay there a moment, trying to pinpoint the sound. When she realized the noise was running water, the reality of her situation crashed in on her. Sleep had lulled her into a happy place where she was her own woman, in her own apartment, with her own job to go to. But no. She was in a strange house, sleeping in a tiny bed—which was surprisingly comfortable, at least—in a closet-sized room. The water running had to be the shower, and the muffled baritone that occasionally broke out in snatches of Keith Urban's *The Fighter* was none other than her ex-husband.

She pried her eyes open and squinted at the vile red numbers on the clock. Four-thirty? Who got up at this hour other than to pee?

The answer arose from memories of growing up on Uncle Fred's farm.

"Farmers," she muttered.

Yesterday he'd caught her by surprise, showing up at her house before she was out of bed. But not today. Today it was her turn to surprise Jason.

She threw her legs over the side of the bed and stumbled three steps to the chest of drawers in the closet. Using the light from her cell phone, she donned a pair of jeans and a tee shirt, ran a brush through her tangled tresses, and twisted them up into a messy knot on top of her head. Then she slipped from her room as quietly as possible.

Last night she'd taken inventory, so she already knew her way around the kitchen. Moving quickly, she made coffee and then she cracked open a tube of biscuits. When they'd been put in the warm oven, she layered thick slices of bacon in a big iron skillet. By the time Jason emerged, freshly shaved and his thick hair still wet, she was whisking eggs with a touch of cream.

He halted in the doorway, surprise etched on his face.

"Good morning," she chirped in a bright voice. "I hope you slept well."

"I—" His mouth slammed shut, and his gaze slid to the sizzling bacon and then to the coffee pot. "I did. And you?"

"Wonderful. That bed is more comfortable than my old one at Fred and Rainey's." The eggs whipped to fluffy readiness, she poured them into a pan with a dash of melted butter. "Have a seat. I'll get you some coffee."

Jessica swallowed a giggle at the suspicious glances he kept throwing her way. Did he think she couldn't handle herself in a kitchen? Maybe that's why he'd suggested this arrangement, so he could watch her fumble and laugh at her failures. Well, she'd prove him wrong.

Anyone who'd been raised by Aunt Rainey knew their way around a farmhouse.

And this one was in serious need of attention. Dusty, musty and downright dirty in some places.

She set a mug of steaming coffee in front of him. "How long has Mrs. Perkins been gone?"

"I told you. A week." He lifted a wary look up at her. "Why?"

A week? Either she wasn't a very good housekeeper, or things have turned into a shambles very quickly.

"Just wondered."

She returned to the stove, flipped the bacon, and stirred the eggs, humming as she worked. *The Fighter,* the same song he'd sung in the shower. A quick glance over her shoulder showed her he noticed, and she smiled at the spots of color rising on his tanned cheeks.

A few minutes later she set a plate of bacon and eggs in front of him. "You get started on that. The biscuits are coming out now."

He picked up his fork, and she noticed his plaid cotton work shirt clung to his skin like Saran Wrap. She walked back to the oven, took out a pan of light, golden-brown biscuits, and placed them on the trivet resting on the table. From the large refrigerator, she removed the juice and butter. As she poured him a glass of juice her gaze returned to his shirt.

"What's the matter with your shirt?" she asked.

He spread generous amounts of golden butter over his flaky, hot biscuit. With a downward glance at his attire, he shrugged his broad shoulders. "Can't figure it out myself." He bit into the steaming biscuit.

"It looks like static electricity." She set her plate in front of a chair on the other end of the table and reached for the honey jar. When she'd smeared an ample amount on the biscuit, she licked her fingers free of the sweet, sticky substance. "Do you do your own laundry?"

"Try to." He grimaced. "It's not one of my favorite

things."

She stood up, reached for the coffeepot, and refilled Jason's thick brown mug with the hot liquid. "Do you use fabric softener when you wash?"

He held his third biscuit in front of his mouth and answered curtly. "I don't know what I use. It's sitting in there on the washing machine in a big box."

Though he was obviously getting tired of the conversation, she persisted.

"That's just the washing powder," she informed him. "Don't you use anything but that when you wash?"

He shot her an impatient look. "No, I just put a cup of that stuff from the blue box in the washing machine and turn it on. When it's through, I put it in the dryer, turn it on 'normal heat,' and press the start button." His voice dropped to a monotone mutter. "Just like Mrs. Perkins told me to."

Jessica shook her head and set down her coffee cup. "Doesn't that bother you, clinging to your skin like that all day?"

"It's irritating," he agreed in a clipped tone.

"Well." She sighed. "I'll do your laundry while I'm here." She picked up her juice glass and took a small sip from it. "To keep everything even, you can clean the drain in the hallway bath. Something really gross is clogging it."

"Great." He shoved the last of the biscuit in his mouth, pushed away from the table, and stood up. He reached for his hat, which hung on the coat rack by the back door of the kitchen.

Hand on the door handle, he paused. "Thanks for breakfast. I usually eat a health bar."

"You're welcome." She smiled. "Have a nice day."

When the door closed behind him, Jessica sat back in her chair and sipped her coffee. She'd caught him off guard this morning. Apparently, he'd expected a return of the snarky, reticent Jessica from last night. But who wanted to live in a constant verbal sparring match for six months? No, since she'd agreed to this arrangement, she might as well make the best of it. A glance around the pleasant kitchen settled a comfortable feeling in her. How often as a teenager had she dreamed that this kitchen would one day be hers? That she would one day live in this house? This had been her dream house for a long time, and this the life she wanted. Living here, cooking for Jason, taking care of his house, raising his children—

With a start, she jerked up right. Coffee slopped over the rim of her mug.

Watch it, Jessica, she cautioned herself. This is a business arrangement only. Nothing personal. Remember that.

But she would always have these memories. No one could take that from her

Exactly one month to the day after Jessica's arrival, the fact that this make-believe life was nothing more than a business arrangement slapped her full in the face.

Balancing the roles of remote corporate executive and housekeeper wasn't as difficult as she'd feared. In fact, she slipped into a new routine quickly. After cleaning up the breakfast dishes, she spent several hours at her laptop and on the phone, handling the day-to-day issues that arose at Fancy Duds. Then she turned her attention to her second job.

The farmhouse had undergone an almost miraculous change. Bright throw pillows and paintings, ordered online, now enlivened the rooms with their vivid splashes of color. Lush green foliage adorned each room throughout the house. Even Jason's prized plant now showed signs of rapidly improving health.

Jessica had washed and ironed all the curtains that now hung freshly starched at the windows and had mopped and waxed the kitchen floor until you could see your face in the finish. She had shampooed the green, plush carpeting in the living room, bedrooms, and hall, bringing back the color to almost new.

Cooking had always been a favorite hobby of Jessica's, but for the first time she was able to throw herself into preparing meals that, while not gourmet, tested her skills and delighted her nearly as much as designing ladies' clothing. She looked forward to the end of every day, when Jason entered the house, stopped, and lifted his head to inhale the mouth-watering smells of the dinner she'd prepared.

He'd looked completely overwhelmed the first time she greeted him with a tall glass of iced tea and his favorite apple pie bubbling hot in the oven.

His clothes now hung, cleaned and pressed, in his closet, buttons all replaced, and his socks were mended and lying neatly in his dresser drawers. He seemed particularly pleased with her mending ability.

"How did you do that?" he'd asked, his fist thrust to the heel in a sock.

She shrugged. "Aunt Rainey taught me."

"Wow."

His expression had been so full of admiration that she was almost embarrassed. "What? It's not that hard."

"When Mrs. Perkins comes back, would you show her? I asked her to mend several pairs once, and for weeks I felt like he was walking on rocks. Now every time I get a hole I throw them away and buy new ones."

Little things like that left Jessica feeling almost giddy. This was a life she could settle into. Until...

They had just finished supper, which Jason had eaten rapidly. He left the room the minute he was done. Sounds of the shower running reached down the hallway as she cleared away the dinner dishes. What his big hurry was tonight?

Fifteen minutes later a red convertible pulled up in the drive and the driver honked the horn.

Jessica peeked out through the kitchen curtain, and her heart sank. In the driver's seat sat a pretty, brown-haired girl who smiled warmly at her. She managed to smile back, then dropped the curtain. The clean, fresh smell of Jason's aftershave filled the room as he walked through the kitchen toward the back door.

He opened the screen. "I may be late. Just leave the back door unlocked."

Jessica watched as he walked out to the red car, leaned down and kissed the driver, then went around to the passenger's side to slide in. The car pulled swiftly out of the driveway in the direction of town.

Sharp pangs of jealously coursed through her as she walked away from the window. Well, what had she expected? There had to be other women in Jason's life. She had no claim on him, not anymore. But it still hurt. She wiped at the unexpected tears that rose in her eyes. Then resentment stabbed at her. How different things could have been, if only she'd had the gumption to stand up to Uncle Fred and Aunt Rainey concerning their marriage.

Wiping ineffectually at the streaming tears, she finished putting the dirty dishes in the dishwasher and switched it on. Turning out the light in the kitchen, she wandered back through the silent house. When she clicked on a small lamp in the living room, her gaze fell on a shirt that Jason had carelessly draped there. She picked it up and hugged it to her cheek. The unique, special smell of Jason assaulted her nostrils, the faint aroma of his aftershave clinging to the soft fabric. Once again, tears wet her cheeks.

What is this? She swiped at her face, impatient with herself. Their relationship was over long ago.

Wasn't it?

Did my feelings for Jason ever really leave?

The answer came in a flash, and she buried her face in the shirt. No. She loved him still. Her slender body shook with the force of her deep sobbing. She loved him more than life itself, but he would never be hers again. He had moved on, and she— Only once in a lifetime could anyone feel the kind of love she felt for Jason. How would she ever bear the pain of losing him again?

It was very late when she finally heard the car pull into the drive. She set aside the book that had failed to keep her attention. With a deep sigh, she reached up and switched off her bedside lamp. Snuggling down under the cover, she heard Jason let himself in the back door, not any too quietly. Banging his way down the hall, she traced his way by his footsteps. When he paused before her door, her breath caught in her throat.

"Jessica?" he whispered. "Are you sleeping?"

"I'm awake." She slid out of bed and pulled on a pair of shorts. "Did you need something?"

"No, I just—"

When she opened the door, his eyebrows arched in surprise.

"You just what?" She twisted her hair in a long braid. "Wanted to wake me up to tell me about your *date?*"

Now that he was back, Jessica suddenly felt very hostile toward him. How dare he go off on a date and have fun, while she sat at home trying to read a stupid book? Hair settled, she pushed past him and padded her way to the kitchen. Maybe a glass of milk would help her sleep.

He followed, and leaned against the doorway. "What did you do this evening?"

"Nothing as interesting as you, I'm sure." She nearly winced at the petulance in her voice.

"How do you know what I did?"

"I guessed." Jessica poured milk into a glass, and

then held the carton toward him in an unspoken question. When he shook his head, she returned it to the refrigerator. "Who was your date?"

His eyes narrowed, and then he answered in a teasing tone. "Monica Sawyers."

"She's very pretty." She gulped the milk. "Have you been dating her long?"

Drat! Why did she ask that? She didn't want to know anything about the woman.

He confirmed her worst fear. "About a year."

"It must be serious." How could her voice sound normal when her chest felt so tight?

"It could be." He avoided her gaze.

She drained her milk. "Well, good night."

"You really ought to get to know Monica, Jessie. She's a nice person." He didn't move, but continued to block the doorway.

Her temper flared. If he launched into a list of Monica's attributes, she'd scream.

"Excellent idea," Jessica said with mock enthusiasm. "Tell you what. Why don't I bake her a cake in my spare time and take it to her?"

One of his eyebrows twitched upward. "You wouldn't by any chance be jealous of her, would you?"

Now it was her turn to avoid his gaze. "Have a nice day, Jason." She tried once again to pass him, but he remained planted.

"You're sure?"

The last of her patience fled. Jessica shoved past him, her patience clearly at an end. "Don't mess with me. Mr. Rawlings. You'll soon learn that I'm not a morning person."

"You know what, ex-Mrs. Rawlings? I believe you *are* jealous."

That crooked smile twitched at his lips, and the sight drained her anger. Jealous? Of course she was jealous. She could spit bullets at the mere thought of

Jason with another woman, but admitting that would give him a weapon against which she had no defense.

She sighed, and stepped close to him. He straightened, suddenly wary.

"I hope Monica and her new husband are very happy together." A bald-faced lie, but she'd never admit it.

She rose onto her tiptoes and planted a light, brotherly kiss on his cheek, then pushed past him. "Enjoy the lovely sunshine. I'm going back to bed."

When she closed the door to her bedroom, he had not moved.

Jessica was sliding a pan of cinnamon rolls in the oven when Jason came into the kitchen the second morning. Without saying a word, he walked over to the coffeepot and poured himself a large steaming cupful before he slid into his chair at the table.

Jessica had spent several sleepless hours wondering how to act this morning. She hadn't seen him when he came in last night. She left his supper in the warming oven with the instructions to put the cat out and turn off the back-porch light. She was in her "room." Avoidance, she'd decided, was the best course, whenever possible. Of course, they would be in close proximity, but if she steered cleared of him, other than business matters, the time would pass more quickly. Whatever had possessed her to kiss his cheek? The act had felt so natural, so good. So utterly foolish. She decided to pretend the slight peck on his cheek never happened. She had been totally out of place.

"Good morning," she said brightly.

"Is it?" Jason grumbled.

"What's the matter? Didn't you sleep well last night?"

His palm slapped the table so hard she jumped.

"What's with the kiss last night? I thought we agreed this was a business arrangement only."

"We did; I lost my head. I'm sorry." She slid the rolls out of the oven. "It will never happen again. Goodness. One little peck on your cheek and you go ballistic."

"It was a kiss." He stiffened in his chair. "And darn inconsiderate of you. This situation is going to be hard enough without you making passes at me."

"Making passes at you!" She slammed the hot pan on the stove top. "You consider a friendly peck making a pass at you?"

He launched himself out of the chair and stalked across the room to stand in front of the patio door. He ran his hands through his thick hair, the muscles in his back tensing.

"I thought I had made it perfectly clear I'm doing you a favor. Nothing more."

The way he spat the last word struck her like a slap.

"Well excuse me all the way to Austin, Mr. Rawlings." It would be a cold day in you-know-where before she'd so much as look at him.

"That's how it starts- one little kiss. Next thing I know, I'll be giving you friendly pecks, and then neighborly hugs and innocent winks and—"

"Calm down and eat your breakfast, toad. I have no plans to 'molest' you ever again."

After a moment's hesitation, he returned to his chair and reached for a roll. "See that you don't."

"Fine." She shrugged. "Do you want bacon with these rolls?"

"No."

He picked up his fork to eat. "Simmer down. I'm sorry I jumped you like that but we need to stick to the agreement. No need to get all bent out of shape

"I'm fine, you're the one bent out of shape." She didn't bother to filter the sarcasm from her voice. She pushed a dish toward him. "Butter?"

He gave her a thin-lipped smile. "Maybe a glass of orange juice?"

"Sure...boss." Though she managed a civil tone, she shoved back from the table, causing his coffee to slosh over his plate.

He snatched up a second roll and shoved back from the table. "Changed my mind. I think I'll clear out."

"Maybe you should. I have floors to mop."

"Yeah—and hit the bathrooms, okay? They need freshening up."

He brushed by her, set his hat jauntily on his head, and stepped out the back door. A moment later he stuck his face through Rainey's open kitchen window. "Remember, hands off the merchandise."

She gave him an *ummpt* face. "God give me strength," she said out loud.

Nine

The Fourth of July dawned hot and muggy. Jessica sat in front of the kitchen fan drinking a glass of tea, and browsed through recipes on her laptop. Two months had passed since she and Jason began their arrangement.

Since the morning of their argument over the innocent kiss, Jason kept a safe distance. Outwardly they laughed and talked, but inwardly Jessica was intensely aware of a tension between them. He must feel it too. And lately Rick Warner had begun to hang around Jessica's doorstep, apparently a source of deep irritation to Jason.

She paged down on the screen, scanning the list. What should she take to the annual picnic and Fourth of July dance? The celebration had been a standing tradition in this small town for over fifty years. In fact, it was the highlight of the year, second only to Christmas. Jessica was especially looking forward to the event having missed so many the past years. She had scheduled some vacations for a trip home, but most were working vacations that took her to Paris, Germany and Italy.

The meal was always served in the open air unless it rained, in which case it was moved to the covered pavilion. The tables groaned under every type of food imaginable, each woman bringing her own particular specialty. Eight years ago, the dinner was viewed as an unspoken contest to see who had the most sought-after recipe at the end of the day. Jessica was sure that friendly competition hadn't changed. Cakes, pies, breads, jams, jellies, fried chicken, hams, big buckets of corn on the cob dripping with homemade butter, freezers of fresh-churned ice cream, watermelons—the list went on and on.

The men would try to out-eat one another, and the women would throw their diets out the window for the day. Having a teenager's metabolism back then, Jessica never had to worry about her weight, but Aunt Rainey used to pay a heavy penalty the rest of the week.

After the meal, when every button on their pants had popped, the old fiddlers would tune up their instruments, along with the guitar and banjo players. Before long every foot would be tapping, hands would be clapping, and couples would pair off for the dance. From then on, the old pavilion would fairly rock on its foundation until around midnight, when the merchants of the town put on a spectacular fireworks display that signaled the end of another happy, successful Fourth.

Then came the job of gathering sleepy, slightly grimy children into parents' arms, rounding up all the empty dishes, and heading for home, tired but happy.

A recipe caught Jessica's eye. What about German

chocolate cake? That always seemed to be a hit wherever she went.

A sound in the driveway alerted her to an approaching vehicle. The engine sounded like Jason's truck. Surprised, she glanced at the clock. She rarely saw him around the house during the day. A door slammed, and a few minutes later he opened the back screen and poked his head in.

"You got a minute, Jessie?"

"Sure." She closed the lid on her computer, got up from the table, and trailed him out into the yard. He'd parked his truck by his tractor. On the ground lay a set of jumper cables.

"The tractor's battery is as dead as a doornail." He shook his head. "Won't even take a jump. I want you to drive the truck. I'm going to try to pull-start it."

The first stirring of panic rose in her throat. "I don't know, Jason. I'm not very good at things like this. Can't you get Sam to help you?"

He spoke curtly. "Sam's plowing a field in the south section today."

"What about Rick?"

"Everyone's busy right now. Just do what I tell you, and you won't have any problems." He walked around to the front of the tracker and hooked up a thick, heavy chain. "Jump in my truck and drive. It'll only take a minute."

She walked slowly to the truck. "I don't think this is such a good id—"

"Just get in it and back it up to the tractor so I can hook this chain on."

The damage she'd inflicted on the pickup the day after Aunt Rainey's funeral had been repaired. No evidence of the mishap remained on the shiny new vehicle. She climbed onto the plush seat and turned the key in the ignition. The motor started up with a smooth sound. Eyes glued onto the rear-view mirror, she carefully backed the truck up to the tractor, her palms sweating. Jason hooked the heavy chain to the back of the truck and jumped up onto the tractor seat, shouting instructions.

"Just give it a little gas, ease off the clutch real slow until you feel the chain go taut, then let off the gas when you hear the tractor start. Got it?"

Sweat trickled down her back. She gripped the steering wheel so hard her knuckles turned white.

"Pull me down toward the barn," he shouted. "Okay, go!"

"Jason." She stuck her head out the truck window for a final plea. "This really makes me nervous."

"Just do it, Jessie." His voice snapped with impatience. "I haven't got time to argue. Are you ready?"

"I guess," she said in a small voice.

"Okay," he ordered. "Go!"

She pressed down on the gas pedal very slowly. The chain made a popping noise, like it was going to tear the whole bumper off the truck. She began crawling down the drive at a snail's pace, perspiration dripping off her face and arms.

"Faster," Jason yelled. "You've got to get up more speed."

"God, I can't do this." She moaned the prayer as she let her foot slip from the gas pedal just a little. The heavy chain immediately went slack.

"Keep it taut!" Jason shouted.

In response, her foot came back down hard on the pedal—too hard. She immediately let up on the gas again. No, wait. That was a mistake. The truck jerked Jason along on the tractor in giant hiccupping jolts.

"Get the slack out, Jessie!" His shout held a note of hysteria now. Her foot slammed down even harder on the pedal, and the truck surged forward. The chain was definitely taut now. Then a loud snap sounded as the chain broke. The truck catapulted straight toward the barn at something just short of the speed of sound.

Oh, no! She fought frantically to bring the vehicle under control. In an instant, the truck became her enemy. She put up a valiant fight, but the truck won. The front end plowed through the side of the barn as easily as a hot knife slicing through butter.

Heart pounding, she glanced around sheepishly for a moment. Shoot. Trying to act nonchalant, she pulled the gear shift into reverse and backed slowly out of the yawning chasm. She hazarded a glance in the rearview mirror. Jason stood up on his tractor, his face a mask of astonishment. Coming out of his state of shock, he leaped off the tractor and ran toward the truck. "Are you hurt?" That sounded like real concern in his voice.

By this time Jessica was shaking like a leaf and feeling like an utter fool—once again.

"No," she said in a shaky voice, "I don't think so."

He let out a long breath and sagged against the truck. He took off his hat and wiped his forehead on his shirt sleeve. Knocking the dust from his hat on his denim-clad leg, he put it back on his head. "I know where we can make a fast buck, Angel. I can rent you out as a one-woman demolition squad."

What nerve! Anger surged, and in an instant, she was as mad as a wet hen. Furious tears sprang to her eyes. "I told you I couldn't do it, but, no, you had to make me try—screaming at me, 'Faster, Jessie, keep the chain taut, Jessie.' You had me so nervous I could have died. Now you have the audacity to stand there and insinuate that it was my fault." She jerked her door open and nearly fell out onto the ground. Regaining her balance, she stiffened her back. "I don't have to stand here and take this."

With the air of a queen going to hold court, she turned and flounced off toward the house, leaving him standing in the rubble.

❧

The sounds of hammering and sawing could be heard as the tantalizing aroma of the chocolate cake drifted from the oven. Through the kitchen window, Jessica watched the wrecker pull Jason's truck out of the farmyard while a ranch hand hammered away on the side of the barn. A feeling of foolishness swept over her again. Even if it wasn't her fault this time, Jason's men probably thought he'd hired a refugee from a mental institution as his housekeeper. It had become a standing joke among his men, the way she systematically went about destroying his vehicles. That was *so* not the way she wanted to be viewed—especially by Jason. Why did she keep humiliating herself in front of him?

She went to the refrigerator and poured a large glass of lemonade, then stepped out through the back door.

Jason approached, his face hot and flushed. "You got an extra glass of that?"

She forced a pleasant tone. "There's a whole pitcher full."

"I was coming in to cool off, and by the sound of things I won't have any trouble." He flashed a boyish grin that set her pulse fluttering.

Jessica dipped her head toward the kitchen. "Go on in. It's nice and cool in there."

He stepped into the kitchen, and then jerked backward so fast he nearly knocked her over. "Holy moly, it's like a furnace in here."

"Isn't it, though?" Jessica forced a serene tone.

"How do you put up with this all day?" He removed his hat to wipe the sweat from his brow.

She poured him a large glass of icy lemonade. "My 'boss' likes big, hot, home-cooked meals, remember?"

Jason grinned sheepishly and took the glass of lemonade from her. "Do you realize the 'boss' has gained ten pounds this month alone on those home-cooked meals?"

With a proud smile, she lowered her gaze to the tiny little tummy protruding slightly over the waist of his jeans. "I'd noticed."

He used his hat as a fan to stir up a breeze on his reddened face. "Why didn't you say something about it being so hot in here? I'm never in the house enough in the daytime to notice. I'll have one of the men put in an air conditioner first thing in the morning."

"I'd be eternally grateful." Jessica dipped her head in acknowledgement.

"You ready for the picnic tonight?" He took another long drink of lemonade.

"Almost." She flipped the oven light on and peered at her cake.

"I'll try to wind things up around four so we can get an early start."

Jessica turned a surprised look on him. "Am I riding with you?"

"How else did you plan on getting there?" A smirk twisted his lips. "Drive my truck?"

She chose to ignore the dig. "I don't know—ride with Rick, I suppose. Aren't you taking anyone?"

Jason stared out the kitchen window toward the hammering down at the barn. "I'm taking you, aren't I?'

A pleased thrill coursed through Jessica. To hide her pleasure, she turned her back on him and removed her cake from the oven. The delicious, rich chocolate aroma permeated the hot kitchen.

He gawked at the cake and inhaled deeply. "Well, that looks like another five pounds. Where did you learn to cook like a pro?"

"Rainey. She says a man has to have the proper fuel to run a farm."

"She was right, as usual." He touched his finger to the frosting.

"Have you ever thought about not eating any?" she

teased.

"Nope, that would be sacrilegious."

A pleased giggle escaped her throat. She had managed to find the way to his stomach. Now if she could just find the way to his heart. The thought startled her. She had managed to keep the relationship of housekeeper/employee on a solid basis without once acknowledging her growing feelings, feelings she thought were long dead. This morning was the first hint of the old Jason.

"Well, back to the old grind." He picked up his hat and shoved it on his head.

On his way to the back door he stopped and turned, his gaze catching hers. Something unreadable lay hidden in the soft green depths of his eyes. She swallowed hard. Oh, how she longed to walk over and kiss him. If they were married, that's exactly what she would do every time he stuck that handsome mug of his in the door.

But they weren't married. Why kid herself into thinking they ever would be again?

"Did you want something else, Jason?" she forced herself to ask lightly.

"No, I was just thinking...." His voice trailed off. "See you tonight, Angel."

Then he was gone, the screen door slamming shut behind him. Her heart swelled with emotion for that irritating, lovable man who had once been hers.

"I'll be waiting," she whispered softly.

Ten

The festivities were in full swing when they pulled up in Jason's Continental that evening. He got the picnic hamper out of the trunk, and they made their way through the crowd of friends and neighbors who shouted their hellos with boisterous backslapping and bone-crushing handshakes.

"Jessica!"

Rick Warner's voice caught Jessica's attention immediately. Beside her, Jason stiffened as Rick bounded up to them, his face a wreath of smiles— all for Jessica.

"Hell-ooo, pretty lady." Jessica had to laugh at his comical elation over her appearance. "I sure hope you brought whatever was making that mouth-watering smell float around in the air this afternoon." He gave a broad wink. "I've been seriously thinking of offering to marry you all afternoon, just to be able to come home to your cooking every night."

Without allowing her the opportunity to reply, Jason took Jessica's arm and propelled her through the picnic grounds.

"Her cake will be on the table along with everyone else's," he tossed over his shoulder.

To her delight, Rick trailed along beside them. "Can she eat a piece of it with me?"

He cast an openly flirtatious glance her way, which made her giggle. Rick obviously wasn't afraid of his boss's grim expression.

"That's entirely up to the 'pretty lady'," Jason said.

"Well, Jessica?" Rick hopped around them and planted his feet squarely in front of her, watching her hopefully.

She pasted on a sweet smile. "I'll make it a point to look you up when I'm ready for dessert, Rick."

Taking her hand in his, he gazed at her adoringly. "I'll be waiting."

Jason walked on through the crowd, pulling her alongside him. "That punk kid gets on my nerves."

"For heaven's sake, he's not a kid. He's my age." She cast a look sideways. Was he jealous? What a delightful idea.

"Then if you two 'kids' want to carry on a flirt-fest, do it when I'm not around," he snapped.

She opened her mouth to deliver a hot retort, then caught herself. Instead, she smiled sweetly. "I'm sorry, Jason. From now on we'll try to control ourselves in your presence. We're animals, you know, so it isn't going to be---"He pulled her along faster.

Jason paused and turned to face her. "Look. Let's not do this tonight. We're supposed to be having fun."

In the face of his open honesty, Jessica's temper receded. She conceded with a dip of her forehead. "You're right. We'll make a pact—no digs or taunts. Not tonight. Deal?" She stuck out a hand.

"Deal." Instead of shaking to seal the deal, he grabbed hers in his left. "Come on. I'm hungry."

Nor did he let go as they walked on through the crowd. Several people stopped to chat with them. While they were talking with the Ramseys, Jessica noticed a young woman standing off to the side, admiring Jason with her big, dark-brown eyes. Her expression resembled that of a child staring into a pet-store window full of puppies. Jessica might have even felt sorry for her, but at that moment Jason glanced at girl. Giving her a nod of greeting, he turned back to the conversation with Mr. Ramsey.

A stab of jealousy tore through Jessica. Would she ever get over the hurt at seeing him with another woman?

The answer lay down deep in her heart. To think of another woman in Jason's arms—where she longed to be more than anything in this world—was like having a knife slice through her soul. While Jason continued his conversation, Jessica slipped quietly away. What she needed was distance, a few minutes to wander through the crowd to calm her mangled thoughts.

Before long everyone began to gather around the tables. An air of contagious joviality swept through the crowd. The lighthearted holiday spirit put smiles on every face. Jessica got in line to fill her plate, noting that Jason and the man he'd been speaking with followed not far behind her.

Though she tried to take only a tiny taste of everything, she soon had enough food piled on the plate that she had to support the bottom with a flat hand. She selected a table and sat down.

Rick brought his plate over and slid in beside her.

"Mind if I join you?"

She smiled. "Not at all."

Across the table, Jason shot her a disagreeable look as he set his plate down. Jessica focused on her food, determined to ignore his presence.

For the next few minutes all thoughts of conversation vanished as the town folk dedicated themselves to the feast spread out before them. Mass quantities of food were consumed. Finally, when not a single soul could stuff one more deviled egg down, they sat around conversing in low tones, catching up on the local gossip.

The women began clearing off the tables, and the musicians started tuning their instruments. Couples grabbed for each other's hands and headed for the pavilion. The really fun part of the night was about to get underway. It would begin with a couple of hours of serious square dancing. When everyone was totally worn out, the pace would slow down for the remainder of the evening.

As Jessica recollected, the pavilion dance floor was usually jam-packed, and tonight was no exception. Apparently, Bob Preston had been tapped to do the calling. He grabbed the microphone and shouted into it, his voice booming through the speakers.

"Now, listen up, folks. We're goin' to get this dancin' underway. Grab your partner."

Couples began forming squares all around the dance floor, and the band started playing "Cotton-Eyed Joe."

Rollicking music filled the air. Beneath the table, Jessica tapped her foot and watched the couples, young and old, two-stepping out onto the dance floor. She glanced around, about to suggest to Rick that they join the dancers, but he'd disappeared somewhere.

Then out of nowhere, Jason stood by her side. "Want to dance the next square?"

"Oh, could we?" She clapped her hands, as excited

as a child on Christmas morning.

His face broke into a wide grin. "I'm game if you are."

For the next two hours, Jessica had more fun than she'd had in years. It felt great to be back home again. She danced every square with a different partner. Once she found herself partnered with Clevon Johnson, who had about as much rhythm as a grade school orchestra. Hopefully he attributed her laughter to her enjoyment of the festivities. When was the last time she'd danced this much? She stopped only long enough to gulp down a glass of cold punch which Jason had handed her during one of the breaks in the music.

"Having fun, Jessie?" Amusement lay softly in the green eyes that held hers.

"I haven't had so much fun in ages." She giggled.

"Yoo-hoo! Jaaaason!"

They both turned to see Marcy Mercy bounding through the couples waiting on the dance floor, dragging Willis along behind her. Jessica had never seen a more mismatched couple in her life. Marcy had not lost any of her beauty. On the contrary, she was lovelier than ever, but Willis—Willis gave a whole new meaning to the word homely. There really wasn't an attractive feature about him. He was short and stocky, with a thatch of coarse red hair sitting on his head like a deserted bird nest. He wore glasses so thick it almost made you dizzy just to stand and talk to him. Marcy and Willis looked like Beauty and the Beast together, but one thing was obvious. Willis adored his wife. Judging by the way Marcy gazed at him, she seemed to return his affection.

"There you are." Marcy called as she neared. "I told Willis I hadn't seen you all night. Where have you been hiding?"

"Hi, Marcy," Jason called to her. Under his breath he said to Jessica, "Stay close. She's like a bad case of poison ivy—hard to get rid of."

"Jessica, you remember Marcy and Willis Mercy, her husband?"

"Certainly," Jessica said. "Hi, Marcy, Willis."

"Jessica! Why, you've hardly changed after all these years." A look of distaste crossed her features. "Still lovely."

Jessica smiled tensely. Yes, the same Marcy she remembered. "Neither have you, Marcy."

"How you doing, Willis?" Jason said.

"Fine, just fine, Jason. Fine night, isn't it? Everything's just going fine."

Jessica frowned. Good heavens, he certainly has a limited vocabulary for a banker.

The music started again. Out of nowhere Rick appeared and grabbed Jessica's hand.

"My turn," he said, flashing a charming grin.

He swept her onto the dance floor and kept her moving at a breathless pace through the steps. One thing about Rick, he could certainly dance. She was happily allemande-lefting when out of the corner of her eye she caught a glimpse of the square directly next to theirs, where Jason danced with a young woman. His lean, lithe body kept perfect time to the music. The woman's face tilted up to his, her eyes shining with undisguised adoration.

A sour feeling settled in her stomach as the night lost all its magic. Jessica's feet faltered in the dance steps.

Rick steadied her with a strong arm. "Whoa, I've got you, pretty lady."

She smiled back gratefully, but her heart was no longer in the dance. They finished the set, and the band swung into a change of pace with the fiddles playing the sweet, lilting refrain of "The Tennessee Waltz." Rick automatically turned her around in his arms and they were gliding back out onto the dance floor when Jason's deep voice rumbled at her side.

"Mind if I cut in?" he asked, respectfully for a change.

"I mind, but since you're the boss..." Grinning with good grace, he handed her into Jason's waiting arms.

As the music washed over Jessica, the magic glow of the evening returned to the dance floor. He held her in a tight embrace, and she lifted her hands around his neck. How many times had they danced like this in the past? Here, in the circle of Jason's embrace, everything felt right. She laid her head on his chest, a deep sigh escaping her lips. This had to be the closest thing to heaven here on earth for her. The fiddles sweetly sang of someone losing their "little darling," but she had hers right here in her arms, if only for the moment.

He guided her effortlessly across the floor, and she inhaled the unique smell of him—his soap, his tantalizing aftershave, the faint, musky smell of sweat. The top of her head didn't quite reach to his chin, and her face nestled into the hollow of his throat as though God had fashioned them to fit together just like this.

The picture of him with Monica, the woman he'd danced with earlier, surfaced in Jessica's mind. Did Monica, too, feel at home in this man's embrace? She drew back, putting space between them.

He looked down at her, surprised. "Are you okay?"

"No," she answered slowly. "Jason, why have you never remarried?"

"Mmmmmmm..." He murmured drowsily, apparently listening to the music. "What brought that on?"

Her head spinning from his nearness, she managed a weak whisper. "Just wondering."

"Why haven't you?" he asked, and pulled her closer.

"I don't know. I guess I haven't found the right man yet." Was it wrong to pray for the music to go on forever?

His voice became husky. "I don't think I want to hear about the rejects."

"There were tons of them," she lied.

"I'll bet there were."

Soft laughter rumbled deep in his chest, and she lifted her head to ask what he found funny. When she did, the words died on her tongue. Her lips were mere inches from his, and she inhaled a giddy draught of his breath. Mesmerized, she watched, transfixed, as his mouth slowly lowered toward hers.

In an instant, her jerked upright. Disappointment flooded through her, like ice surging through her veins.

"I—. Sorry." He shook his head, and then his chest heaved with a rueful laugh. "I've had too much sugar. I'm hyper."

"Excuse me?" Disappointment threatened to give way to ire as she felt her hackles begin to rise. "Afraid someone—like Monica, will see us?"

He gave a short laugh. "Don't go getting yourself in a snit over Monica. She hasn't got a contract on me—yet."

Yet? She wanted to sob. Instead, she let her temper take over. "We wouldn't want that, would we?" She tried to draw away from him, but he held her in an unbreakable hold. Unless she wanted to cause a scene, she couldn't escape. Over his shoulder she caught sight of Marcy watching them.

Calm down, Jessica. The whole town's watching.

She forced a calm tone. "I'm not in a snit, as you call it. I'm just a little surprised. If you were mine, I certainly wouldn't want you dancing with every woman in the room."

He threw his head back and laughed loudly this time.

"What?" She glanced around, a little hurt. Was he laughing at her?

"It strikes me as funny you'd see it that way. I used to be yours, and you casually tossed me away in favor of your aunt and uncle. What did you expect me to do, Jessica, wait until you decided there were things more important in life than going to school and starting a business?"

Rebellion raised its head. Was he saying she shouldn't have pursued an education, shouldn't have launched her business? She stiffened.

He must have sensed the coming explosion, because he hastened to speak before she could. "Besides, what difference does it make to you who I dance with? We have no ties anymore. You've had your share of fun with Rick this evening. Remember, honey, this is just a business arrangement. When the six months are over, I'll take my thirty grand, and we'll part company. Isn't that what we agreed on?"

Her heart sank. He had her there. She had said that. Why was her mind always in neutral and her mouth always in gear?

The band switched to another waltz, her opportunity to escape. But Jason drew her closer and together they glided around the dance floor, which was lit by hundreds of tiny multicolored lights strung around the pavilion.

Since he'd brought up the money, that seemed like a much safer topic of conversation.

Ensuring there was a safe distance between them, she tilted her head up. "Have you thought of what you're going to do with all your money?"

Jason tensed slightly and asked in a cautious tone, "All what money?"

"All of the thirty thousand dollars you're going to have." That had bothered her. What was he going to do with that much money? "Have you given it any serious thought?"

He nodded, his expression solemn.

"Well?" she prompted. "What are you going to do with it?"

"Well, the first thing I'm going to do is take part of it down to the bank and change it into hundred-dollar bills."

"Yes, and then…"

"Then I'm going to take up smoking cigars. I'll carry those hundred-dollar bills around in my pockets to light my cigars with."

She jerked back from his arms, looking directly into his serious, steady gaze. "You're what?"

"I'm going to pull out those hundred-dollar bills and light my cigars with them." He shrugged. "I've always hoped to one day have money to burn."

Surely, he wasn't serious. But he certainly *looked* serious.

She stopped dancing and looked up at him. "Have you gone mad? Totally off your rocker?"

Now his innocent expression took on a touch of mockery. "You said to consider it my 'mad money,' remember?"

The excited shouts of children filled the air as the merchants began their elaborate fireworks display, a signal that the evening was about to draw to a close. Jason led Jessica to a soft grassy spot in the open field and spread out an old army blanket he had retrieved from the back of his truck. With a dramatic gesture, he fell spread-eagled on his back on the blanket in mock exhaustion. She had to laugh at his exaggerated pose, lying there on the ground.

"Let's call a cease-fire for the rest of the night, Angel." He sat up and patted the blanket next to him. "Join me?"

She cocked her head. "Depends. Where's Monica?"

"She left earlier."

Though warning bells tolled in her ears, Jessica dropped to the ground, careful to keep a cautious distance between them.

He heaved a lazy sigh. "Isn't this better?"

She had to admit, getting off her feet felt great. "Much." She lay back beside him and gazed up into the black, clear, beautiful sky. The stars hung so close to the ground she felt she could reach out and touch one of them. The moon had just risen, and cast soft, white beams over the dark shadows of this mystical night.

A favorite childhood song drifted softly through her mind as she gazed into the heavens trying to recall the words. Something about the stars being little candles, and the angels lighting them at night.

Hushed *oohs* and *ahhhs* came from the people around them as the magnificent exploding missiles showered overhead in a blinding array of brilliant colors. Multi-hued sparkles drifted lazily back to earth. A deep feeling of contentment settled over here. Lying here, with the man she loved mere inches away from her, watching the heavens explode...this felt like home in a way Austin never would. If there were ever a time in her life when she had been more content or at peace with the world, she didn't remember it. If she could stop time right here, right now, she would happily do so. But that wasn't possible. Instead she breathed a silent word of thanks to the Lord for having been given this one precious night with Jason, to carry in her dreams for the rest of her life.

Jason stirred beside her, planted his elbow and propped his hand on his chin. "Penny for your thoughts."

She hid a smile. He wasn't given to clichés, which meant...what? Was he feeling a touch of nerves too?

"I was just thinking what a wonderful night this has been." To her astonishment, a tear rolled from her eye and trickled down her cheek. Why did this have to end? If she could have her heart's desire, at this moment it would be to stay here forever, just like this, stretched out next to Jason. She wanted him to protect her, love her, cherish her, for the rest of her life. All her old dreams rushed back to her, as strong now as they were then. She wanted to have his children, grow old with him, play with their grandchildren together—she wanted a marriage like Judge Baker and Wilma, who after nearly fifty years still loved each other with the intensity of newlyweds. Maybe more deeply than newlyweds. They knew the value of true love, a love that could endure for over half a century. Whereas she had given up her only opportunity for a love that strong. In a few months, she would be back in Austin, alone, with only a dream to comfort her.

Another tear followed the first, and she rolled away from him to hide her face.

His whisper tickled her ear. "Why are you crying?"

"I'm not," she insisted.

"You've always been a terrible liar." He laid a warm hand on her arm. "That's the second time today I've made you cry, and I didn't mean to either time, sweetheart."

The endearment stirred up a torrent of more tears, which she fought down. She would *not* sob in front of him. Drawing in deep, shuddering breaths, she grappled with self-control until she could turn over and face him again. An explosion in the sky above painted his face in green and blue flickers.

"I know you didn't." She managed a trembling smile. "And I didn't mean to wreck your truck. It's just that you seem to bring out the worst in me at times." Her gaze lifted to a dazzling display amid the stars, and she spoke quietly. "I'm sorry about your barn, too."

In a rare moment of honesty, he shook his head, his gaze seeking hers. "It's all right, Angel. I shouldn't have made you drive the truck when you told me you didn't want to."

Why did he insist on using that old nickname? Every time he did, a thrill vibrated her insides and drove her nearly to distraction. She gave her head a quick shake.

"The funny thing is, I could have done it for anyone

else. It's only when I get around you that everything always goes wrong." A foot or so of space lay between them, but even so she felt the pull of his body as if he were a magnet and she a paper clip. In an attempt to lighten the mood, she gave a light laugh. "You must think I'm a total idiot."

If anything, his gaze grew even more serious, more intimate. "I've thought a lot about you over the years." His whisper barely reached her ears, low and husky. "But I promise, I've never thought you were an idiot."

The sky exploded in a rainbow finale of pops and sizzles and loud bangs. Applause erupted from the onlookers, and served as a reminder that they were not alone. Reluctantly, Jessica hefted herself up into a sitting position and clapped along with the rest.

Jason helped her to her feet, and then picked up the blanket. Shaking it free of debris, he folded it into a neat bundle. "It's late. We need to go home."

Heaving a sigh, she took one last look at the pavilion and picnic grounds, with their twinkling lights hanging in the soft night. "I wish it didn't have to end."

"I think it's better that it does," he muttered softly. When she lifted a questioning gaze to his face, his lips twitched in a melancholy smile. "We would have made a great team, Angel. Too bad things had to work out like they did."

Eleven

The phone rang bright and early the following morn-ing.

Jessica answered with a cheery, "Hello?"

A pause on the line. "Uh, hi." No mistaking that voice. Jessica's stomach soured. "Is, uh, Jason there?"

Normally he wouldn't be here at this time of day, but he happened to have just walked through the back door and announced that his morning chores were finished. Without a word to the caller, she extended the cordless to Jason.

"For me?" he said, a puzzled look on his face.

'Monica,' she mouthed, and then practically shoved the phone at him.

She returned to her tiny bedroom and began dressing for church. Though she didn't want to eavesdrop, she couldn't stop herself from straining to listen to the rich timbre of his baritone as he laughed at some comment Monica had apparently made. She looked in the mirror and mimicked his laughter, a sarcastic smirk on her face, while jealousy shot through every part of her body. In the next instant, she threw her hairbrush onto the bed with more force than necessary. What was she going to do? With every day she lived here it became more apparent that Jason would never give her a chance again.

But I still love him, she told her reflection, which now held a pitiful feeling-sorry-for-myself expression that sickened her. Over the months since she moved in, their relationship had been a roller coaster, but one thing was certain - her love for him grew every day. Being in his home, seeing him every day, cooking for him, taking care of him—all these things fed the tender blossom of her love. How would she ever be able to give him up again?

Slumping to the bed, she battled tears, something that happened far too often of late. Monica was such a nice person—why couldn't Jessica simply reconcile herself to the fact that eventually Jason would marry her? She would probably make him very happy. The mental image of Monica wrapped in Jason's arms at night tormented her, and a groan escaped her parted lips. What could she do to stop that from happening?

A million thoughts circled her brain, but she dismissed them one by one. Frustrated, she snatched up the hairbrush and jerked it through her tresses. Surely there was something she could do. After all, he had been attracted to her years ago. A flicker of the old flame remained, she'd seen it in his eyes last night. His comment, about what a good team they could have made, might mean he harbored *some* feelings for her.

If so, he sure kept it hidden lately. He went out of his way to avoid her. Last night's Fourth of July picnic was a fluke. Most of the time he treated her the same as he would treat Mrs. Perkins.

She jerked the edge of her quilt to straighten it. No, she just couldn't sit idly by and let him slip through her fingers again without trying to win him back. But short of stepping over boundaries she couldn't force herself to cross, how? First, she had to make him spend time with her, and he didn't—

An idea materialized. She stared at herself in the mirror as it became a full-fledged plan. A mischievous glint came into her eyes. What could she do to entice him to spend some time with her alone?

From the kitchen, his voice droned on while she wracked her brain to come up with an idea. Short of her death, what could she do to keep him home? Hmmm. Maybe not death, but what about near death? A triumphant grin spread across the face reflected in the mirror. She wiped it away, and hurriedly un-made the bed she'd just straightened. With both hands she mussed her hair, and then used her fingers to smear her eyeliner into the tender skin beneath her eyes. She cracked open her door in time to hear him bid Monica goodbye, and made a dash for the bed.

A whistle betrayed his location as he came down the hall. He came to a stop in front of her room, and tapped with a knuckle.

She adopted a weak tone. "Come in."

The door opened, and a smiling Jason stuck his head inside. "I'm going on a picnic. See you later, okay?"

"Sure. Have a wonderful time, Jason," she muttered, and drooped her eyelids partially closed.

Concern overtook his features. "Hey, you feeling all right?"

She let out a shuddering breath. "I'm fine—just fine. But before you go, could you bring me an aspirin?"

He stepped into the room. "An aspirin? Are you sick?"

Eyes fluttering open, she managed a pitiful smile. "I don't know what happened. I was feeling fine a few minutes ago."

Jason walked over and laid a cool hand on her forehead. "You don't seem to have a fever. Where do you hurt?"

"Everywhere—my stomach—my head—even my bones feel achy. I wonder if that sausage I cooked for breakfast was bad. Do you feel okay?"

He shrugged. "I'm fine. I hope you're not coming down with a virus or something."

"Oh, gosh, me too." She released a long, tremulous sigh. "But don't let me keep you. If you could just bring me that aspirin, and maybe a glass of water, I'll be fine." She allowed her eyelids to flutter shut before delivering a well-aimed blow. "If I need anything, I'll call Rick."

She knew without looking that the last dart hit its mark.

"I'm not going to leave you here if you're sick. I'll call Monica back and tell her I can't make it today."

Jessica opened one eye as he turned and started for the kitchen. "Oh, Jason, no." She assumed a valiant tone. "I don't want to spoil your day. I'd feel just awful."

He turned around and awarded her a stern look. "I'm not leaving you, Jessie, and that's final."

A thrill of triumph shot through her, which she carefully concealed. Instead, she released another sigh. "Whatever you say. I'm too sick to argue."

He left the room to make his phone call. When his apologetic tone drifted to her from the kitchen, she felt a twinge of guilt. *This really is a dirty trick to pull on him.* But really, what choice did she have? Her cause was desperate.

A few minutes later he returned carrying a tray,

which he tried to set on the tiny night-stand. Encountering difficulty with the lamp and alarm clock, he instead set it on the foot of the bed. She lifted her head to glance in that direction, and hid a grin. The surface of the tray was crowded with aspirin, Alka-Seltzer, a variety of cold-and-flu medicines, a can of Sprite, a glass of ice, and a folded washcloth.

"I don't' know what'll help, but I've got everything I could think of." He waved at the assortment.

Exhibiting every sign of weakness, she managed to prop herself up on one elbow long enough to swallow an aspirin tablet and wash it down with a sip of soda. "That'll be fine. Thank you." She cast a grateful, almost simpering, glance up at his face. "I appreciate you taking such good care of me."

He insisted that she lay down and placed the cool cloth on her forehead.

"There you go, Angel," he said in a voice more tender than she'd heard in over eight years. "You try to get some sleep. I'll be nearby if you need me."

When he left, he pulled her door almost closed, his gaze fixed on her face the entire time.

Jessica lay back and indulged in a smile. This was exactly where she wanted him – here with her. Not on a picnic with the lovely Monica, but waiting on Jessica, concerned about her, his every thought fixed on her. Only...now that she had him here, what was she going to do with him?

Over the next hour or so she pretended to doze while a variety of intriguing noises filtered into her room. Every so often the banging and scraping would stop, and she would slam her eyes shut just in time when Jason shoved his head through the half-open doorway to check on her. Once she managed a weak request.

"Could I have a glass of juice? I think there's some apple juice in the fridge."

"Of course."

The speed with which he filled her order brought a private smile to her face. But then he returned to whatever noisy task he'd begun.

Two lazy, boring hours passed. Jessica silenced her cell phone and downloaded a silly game to pass the time. Whenever the noise ceased, she shoved the phone beneath the covers and feigned sleep, only to return to it when he left.

The afternoon was half-over when he stepped into her tiny room once again. "Angel?" he asked quietly. "Are you asleep?"

Adopting a pitiful tone, she managed to utter, "Not really. My stomach hurts too badly to sleep."

"Good. Uh—" He held up a hand. "Not good that your stomach hurts, but good that you're not asleep. Do you think you can handle a short walk?"

Curiosity piqued, she managed to tamper down her enthusiasm for something—*anything*—to break the boredom. "If you'll let me lean on you, I think I can manage that."

"Excellent."

He entered the room and helped her untangle her legs from the quilt. Leaning heavily on his strong arm, she let him lead her out of her cell.

"Where are we going?" she asked.

"You'll see in a second."

Excitement danced in his eyes, and his grin looked like a little boy's. It was all Jessica could to not to match his enthusiastic grin. Instead, she focused on leaning heavily on his arm and limping like a weakened invalid down the hallway.

He stopped in front of the room that had once been his, and turned a wide smile on her. "My lady, welcome to your new boudoir."

With a flourish, he swept the door open. The unidentified noises became clear when Jessica stepped inside. The room, into which she had peeked many times in the past few months, glowed with a welcome atmosphere that warmed her heart. Gone were the piles of memorabilia and items belonging to his parents. Even the utilitarian gray bed linens had been exchanged for a white, lacy comforter. The dresser and chest gleamed with fresh polish, and a huge bouquet of wild flowers sat on one of the nightstands, casting a rainbow of goodwill and comfort around the room.

"I..." The words stumbled over a dry tongue. Tears filled her eyes, making his toothy grin a blurry image. "You can't mean this is for *me*?"

His arm slipped around her waist. "Of course it's for you, Angel. And long past time, too." He ducked his head. "I'm sorry for leaving you in that tiny space for so long. I didn't actually mean to."

Emotion overwhelmed her as her gaze circled the room. "Jason, you—" She swallowed past a sob. "You have no idea how much this means to me. Thank you."

"You're welcome." With pressure from his arm, he guided her toward the four-poster bed. "Let's get you settled so you can go back to sleep. I'll move your things in a minute."

She allowed him to guide her to the bed, and stood watching as he peeled back the comforter. As she slid between the crisp, clean-smelling sheets, a wave of dismay washed over her. This was *Jason's* bed, the one he'd occupied while dating her all those years ago. The one he'd slept in the night of their short-lived wedding.

Once enthroned in Jason's bed, Jessica leaned back against fluffy pillows and watched as he transferred her few belongings from the smaller bedroom to this one. Watching him hang her dresses, and carefully lay her clothing in the elaborate chest-of-drawers, she couldn't help but admire his lithe body. This day had turned out far better than she'd hoped. Instead of lounging in a field of wildflowers with Monica, he was here, waiting hand-and-foot on her.

A sudden wave of guilt weighed her down.

"Jason."

He turned from his task of settling a drawer of her tee-shirts, with a quizzical expression.

"I appreciate this." She waved a hand to include the room and the closet and the dresser. "All of it. And you especially."

The crooked grin appeared, the one that made her heart flutter. "It's the least I can do, Angel. Especially after you've taken such good care of me."

"I—" She bit down on her lip. "I feel like I'm taking advantage of you. After all, you're running Uncle Fred's farm too."

He slid the drawer shut and crossed the room to grab a low-backed chair, which he set by the bedside, turned around backward, and straddled. "Don't forget, you're paying me."

"Thirty thousand dollars," she said.

He nodded. "And no cents."

He must really need the money to take on such a project. She hadn't given it much thought before this moment.

Cocking her head sideways, she studied him. "All that stuff about lighting your cigars with hundred dollar bills. You were just messing with me, right?"

"What do you think?" A grin created a pair of delightful dimples in his cheeks. "Nobody would be that stupid, would they?"

She settled back in the pillows. "Definitely not you."

"Oh?" Green sparks appeared in his eyes. "You think I'm smart, do you?"

A giggle stirred deep in Jessica's stomach. This was more like it. Exactly what she hoped would happen when she faked this fatal illness to keep him from his date from Monica. This flirtatious back-and-forth was much more conducive to reigniting a latent spark of love than the silence that had rested between them lately.

She cocked her head and adopted a coquettish grin. "Let's just say I'd be disappointed in you if you were that dumb."

His expression grew serious. "I hope you're not disappointed in me, Jessie."

She was still trying to decide how to respond when he stood. "How about I fix us some soup?"

"Great., I'm starved." Jessica said eagerly Jason's face took on a surprised look. *Oops. Forgot to play the role!* "Uh, I mean... I may be able to force something down."

Suspicion darkened his gaze and he stared at her a moment. She made a point of rounding her eyes and not blinking.

Finally, he jerked a nod. "I'll be right back."

By the time he brought the soup, Jessica was ravenous. She'd only eaten a piece of toast for breakfast and no lunch, but she felt like she'd gulped down at least forty-five aspirins. She had to force herself not to ask for a third bowl of soup.

Jason sat watching her eat with gusto, a knowing smile on his face. "Do you want my bowl?"

Jessica looked up sheepishly. "I think I'm feeling better."

"Obviously," Jason said dryly.

Laying her spoon down carefully on the tray. "I'm through."

He cleared the tray away, then returned to his chair. "Do you want to watch TV?" He inclined his head toward the small TV screen on the dresser.

Did he want to get her interested in a television program so he could sneak off to Monica's? No way Jessica would let that happen, after she'd worked so hard to keep him here today.

"Will you watch with me?" she asked.

Instead of answering, Jason studied her for a moment. "You're looking better. Maybe whatever you had has passed."

"Uhhhhh." She clutched her stomach and moaned. "I don't think the soup is sitting well. It tasted good going down, but I think I overdid it."

Concern returned, and he placed a hand on her forehead. "If it will make you feel better, I'll watch with you."

"Okay," she managed in a weak voice. "You pick. I don't feel up to making a decision."

He settled on an old Disney outdoor film. Jessica considered suggesting that they move to the living room couch so she could snuggle closer to him, but that might be pushing her story of illness a bit far. Instead, Tabby leaped up onto the bed and cuddled up against her side. She had to be content with stroking the cat's soft fur.

The movie drew them both in. By nine o'clock Jessica was starving again. "Doesn't popcorn sound good?"

He turned an astonished gaze on her. "You want greasy popcorn?"

Oops. Pay attention to your role, Jessica!

"Maybe just a small bowl," she said weakly. "Just to see how my stomach handles it."

"Whatever this sickness is, it sure hasn't affected your appetite." He headed for the kitchen.

Oh, how her body ached. Her stiff muscles protested the hours of inactivity. While he was gone, she bounded off the bed to do some quick calisthenics. Tabby awoke from his slumber for a moment, raised his head to watch her, and then, uninterested, went back to sleep. A few seconds of vigorous jogging-in-place felt wonderful. Just what she needed. Then on to arm-stretches.

She was in the middle of her leg kicks when Jason walked back into the room, carrying a large bowl of popcorn and two Cokes.

A snide smirk settled on his features. "Well, hallelujah! I've witnessed a miracle." He set the popcorn down on the bed.

A crimson blush overtook Jessica's face as she slid beneath the sheets. Drat! She thought it would take him longer to make popcorn. Why hadn't she listened more closely for his footsteps in the hall?

"I'm feeling much better all of a sudden," she muttered.

He cocked his head sideways, subjecting her to a scrutinizing stare. "Tell me the truth. You never have been sick, have you?"

Jessica plucked at a loose thread on the quilt, answers warring in her mind. Finally, she heaved a sigh. "Jason, I can't lie to you. No, I haven't been."

His eyes narrowed. "This whole day was a put-on, wasn't it? You didn't want me to go out with Monica today. Is that right?"

Time to let the cat all the way out of the bag. "Yes," she admitted.

His gaze became stony. "That's a pretty rotten thing for you to do."

"But, Jason—"

"No buts, Jessica. That was rotten, pure and simple." He whirled away.

"Jason Rawlings, you come back here," She shouted as he stomped to the door. "I just wanted to spend some time alone with you, you...." She sputtered to a stop, unable to think of a suitable name to call him.

At the door, he turned to face her. "Next time, ask me." He gave her a mock salute and slammed the bedroom door.

"Of all the nerve!"

She bounded out of bed, her temper simmering, and flung her pillow against the closed door. A moment later she heard the rumble of his truck's engine outside. Racing to the window, she arrived in time to see the spray of gravel in the moonlight as he tore down the driveway.

Torn between the desire to cry and to rage, she

slumped down into the chair he'd just vacated. Time was running out. Before long their business arrangement would end, and she'd have to head back to Austin.

That thought drove the rage from her, and tears prickled in her eyes. The truth was, she'd come to a discovery without even realizing it. She didn't want to go back to Austin. The telecommuting arrangement was working out well. Why couldn't it continue? Between Barb and Celeste, they represented her wishes in the day-to-day operations of Fancy Duds.

What she really wanted was for Jason to confess his love for her and ask her to stay. To step into the future she'd dreamed of, the one she walked away from eight years ago. But could she make him love her again?

She straightened in the chair. Jessica Cole, what's the matter with you? It's not like you to throw in the towel.

She wasn't about to give up this easy! There was more than one way to skin a cat.

"No offense," she told Tabby.

Tomorrow was another day, and she had a few more feminine wiles to wield.

Time was running out, and she was a desperate woman.

Twelve

The next day dragged by as she plotted her course of action for that evening. She gave herself a manicure, pedicure, facial—everything she could think of to make her mission less likely to fail.

Late in the morning the home phone shrilled. Jessica ran to answer it, fanning her hands in the air to dry the coat of fingernail polish she had just applied.

Monica Sawyers' lilting voice drifted sweetly over the line. "Jessica?"

Something close to panic threatened to bloom in her chest. Was Monica calling to involve Jason in any plans for this evening?

"Yes?"

"How are you this morning? Jason said you had taken quite suddenly ill yesterday." Her voice held real concern.

Good grief. Why couldn't Monica be the nasty kind of woman she could readily dislike?

Instead she was a super nice person. Under other circumstances, she and Jessica could easily have been friends.

Jessica tempered her voice and said meekly into the receiver. "I'm feeling much better this morning."

"I'm happy to hear that. Are you sure there isn't anything I can do for you?"

You could take a slow boat to China. Shame stabbed at her for the catty thoughts "No, nothing."

"Well, don't hesitate to let me know if you need anything." Monica paused. "I really mean that, you know."

"I know, and thank you for your concern."

A brief moment of silence followed on the line. "Jessica, I wonder if you'd mind answering a nagging question for me. One that's been bothering me a lot lately."

She swallowed hard as she heard the tone of seriousness in Monica's voice. "I wouldn't mind. What is it?"

Another hesitant pause. "I really don't know any way to put this, so I'll just be blunt. Do you and Jason still care for each other?"

Jessica sank down in the chair next to the phone. The frank question left her shaken.

Monica continued, speaking rapidly. "I know about your brief marriage, and I know how hard Jason took the annulment." Her voice dropped. "At times, I really have to wonder if he's completely over you."

"I don't think you have any worries about that." To her dismay, sadness colored Jessica words.

"Don't misunderstand me. I have no intention of prying into your private affairs, and I can readily see how hard it would be to get over a man like Jason. I know. I've fallen in love with him myself. But, I can honestly say I don't know if he returns that love."

Jessica mulled over Monica's words. How right she

was. It wasn't easy getting over a man like Jason.

"I'm not blind," Monica continued. "I see the look that comes into his eyes when your name is mentioned. It seems he's constantly fighting within himself to stay away from you."

The honesty with which Monica was entrusting Jessica with her blunt thoughts touched her. Woman-to-woman, what could she do but return the trust?

Though it hurt her to say the words, Jessica answered in a matching blunt tone. "Jason doesn't want to become involved with me again."

"And, what about you?" Monica asked softly.

"I—I still love him," Jessica admitted.

"But you really feel he doesn't want to get involved again?"

"That's what he's told me on a number of occasions." She shut her eyes against the pain that admission brought.

Monica's voice came calmly back across the line. "Jason's quite a man. You never really know what he's thinking, but somehow I suspect he's not as over you as he believes he is."

Jessica's breath caught in sharp surprise at Monica's remark. "I thought you were in love with him."

"Oh, I am." Monica laughed shakily. "And as much as I like you, you can rest assured I will do everything in my power to keep him. But I can't fault you for loving him, too."

Jessica smiled, shaking her head unbelievingly. Was that a gauntlet being thrown? "Then you won't mind if I do everything in my power to get him back?"

"I'd mind," Monica said. Then her voice took on a cheerful tone. "Let's just say, may the best ma—woman win!"

Jessica matched her friendly adversary's tone. "Thanks, Monica. I'm sure going to try."

As she replaced the receiver in the cradle, her wet

fingernail bumped the hard plastic. "Drat!" she muttered as she bounded for her room to reapply her polish.

At four o'clock she checked the pot roast—one of Jason's favorites—and, satisfied that it would be succulent and tender, headed for the bathroom. She ran a tubful of hot water and sprinkled in the most pleasant-smelling bubble bath from her bathroom vanity. She lay back and relaxed in the aromatic heat, long enough for the fragrance to penetrate her skin.

Her bath finished, she applied her makeup with care. Jason didn't like overly-made-up women. Instead, he preferred a clean, natural look. Jessica had been blessed with smooth, peachy skin, so she contented herself with a bit of powder and focused on her best feature – her eyes. The finishing touch was a bit of slightly-tinted lip gloss. When she was satisfied that she looked her best, she raced back into her bedroom to don the dress she'd selected earlier and laid out in readiness on the bed.

Tabby had made himself a comfy bed in the middle of the silky garment.

"Scat, you pesky cat!"

She shooed him away and applied a lint roller to rid the dress of a layer of hair, and then slid it over her head. The skirt fell in graceful folds to float around her knees. Settling the fabric on the curves of her hips, she turned to face the mirror.

She let out an audible gasp. The pastel violet accented her eyes and hair perfectly, as she'd known they would. But the neckline! It dipped to a dangerous level, showing more cleavage than she was accustomed to revealing. This might be carrying things a little far. Her yellow dress was flattering...

No. She wanted to look as attractive to Jason as she possibly could tonight. Tugging at the neckline, she turned around slowly, looking at every angle in the mirror. The silky fabric clung to her tiny waist, another of her good features. The full skirt barely hinted at soft curves from the rear view. Sweat dampened her palms. Would Jason think she was trying to seduce him?

Was she trying to seduce him?

No. She shook her head. But attract his attention? You bet. Time for him to think of her as a woman instead of just a housekeeper. A kiss would be oh-so-nice....

She ran a hairbrush through her loose, softly curled hair. For the crowning touch, she selected a bottle from her perfume tray that matched the scented bubble bath. Summer Night Love. Just a dab behind her ears and on her wrists.

One last check in the mirror, and she strolled with confidence back to the kitchen. Just in time to put the apple pie in the oven.

Jason was late getting home, and entered the house hot, tired, and dirty. He barely mumbled a greeting and headed immediately for the shower.

Dismayed, Jessica paced the floor. Not a single comment about her dress. Or even about the wonderful aroma wafting from the oven. Had all her efforts been for nothing?

When she heard the shower turn off, she set the food on the table. Pot roast, potatoes, carrots, homemade rolls, a special salad with strawberries and candied pecans. Then she lit candles and dimmed the lights.

He entered the room still rubbing moisturizer on his newly-shaven face, and stopped short. His eyes went round, and she followed his gaze as it took in the candles, the table, and finally rested on her. Her worries fled when appreciation flooded the emerald depths.

"You've been busy today." His eyebrows arched. "What's the occasion?"

"Nothing special." She poured nonchalance into her tone and smiled. "I just felt like dressing up and having a nice meal."

His gaze swept her again, coming to rest on her low neckline. "Well, you look..." He swallowed. "Great."

She brightened her smile. "Thank you."

"I feel underdressed." He glanced down at his jeans and tee-shirt. "Should I change."

With a low chuckle, she shook her head. "You look fine. Let's just enjoy dinner. Maybe afterward we could sit on the porch and watch the stars come out."

Back in the old days, when he still loved her, they would take his car out into the country, lay on the hood with their backs resting on the windshield, and watch the heavens light up.

He gave her a suspicious look, but instead of replying, crossed the floor to the table and pulled out her chair with a gentlemanly gesture.

Pleased, she slid into it.

Dinner progressed with little talk, but Jessica relished in his obvious enjoyment of the food she'd prepared. His gaze returned again and again to her low-cut dress, and more than once heat flooded her face. But he didn't comment, so neither did she.

When she placed a slice of apple pie a la mode in front of him, he caught her wrist and looked deeply into her eyes.

"Thank you. This is the best meal you've cooked since you got here."

She poured warmth into her voice. "You're welcome. I'm glad you enjoyed it."

When she returned to her chair, he appeared to remember something.

"By the way, I saw Willis Mercy today. I invited him and Marcy for dinner tomorrow evening. I hope you don't mind. Since I have to do a lot of business with him at the bank, I try to take them out for dinner every couple of months or so. I just thought it would be nice this time to show off my pretty housekeeper and what she's done with the house." He gestured with his fork toward the pie. "Not to mention her cooking,"

A black cloud came up and hovered momentarily over Jessica's head. "I have to cook dinner for Marcy Evans?"

"No, Angel," he said patiently. "For Marcy Mercy, my banker's wife."

"Same difference," she muttered under her breath, then added quickly, "No, I don't mind. I could do that."

"Good, I thought you could." He made a move as if to leave the room.

When he finished his pie, he stood and patted his stomach. "Too many more like that, Angel, and I'll have to buy bigger jeans." He turned toward the door. "Guess I'll catch up on some of my bookwork before turning in."

He was escaping!

She leaped up from her chair. "Uh, what about the stars?"

Slowly, he turned back to her, his expression guarded. "I don't think that's a good idea."

She crossed the distance between them slowly, giving her skirt a twitch so it would float gracefully. She'd seen that done on TV in an old movie. "It's early yet." Raising her hand slowly, she reached up to smooth the collar of his shirt.

Jason backed away slightly, his eyes locked on the plunging neckline of her dress.

"Is there anything special you'd like to do?" She whispered, a little breathless at her own boldness. What would she do if he suggested...something she wasn't willing to do? "I mean for dinner tomorrow night." She widened her eyes and blinked.

He shifted nervously. "Oh, I don't know." A bead of sweat appeared on his forehead. "Whatever you want."

She moved even closer, rising on her tiptoes to put her lips within kissing range of his. "What I really want is to spend the evening with you." One eyebrow twitched upward. She lowered her voice to a husky tone. "After all, you told me to ask you if I wanted to spend time with you. Didn't you?"

They stood so close she savored the manly smell of his aftershave. His breath warmed her lips.

"What is that perfume you're wearing? It's... really nice," he whispered hoarsely.

"I don't remember." A gleeful thrill coursed through her. His breath came in short, shallow gasps as he reacted to her nearness. This was going to be even easier than she had imagined.

He moved slightly closer. Now his lips were an inch from hers. "Do you want to know what I really want?"

"Tell me." She tilted her head, her sensitive lips aching to feel the touch of his. Her eyes fluttered closed.

"Meatloaf," he whispered softly.

She bit her tongue as her eyes snapped open. "Meatloaf?"

"Yeah, meatloaf. For dinner tomorrow. It's one of my favorites."

The words doused her like a bucket full of ice water. She stepped back, and hastily tugged up her neckline.

His smile twisted into a knowing smirk. He'd known what she was doing and played along just to embarrass her. Fury burned in her face.

"Maybe a few potatoes, a nice big salad, some of those hot rolls you make—you know, just the usual stuff." He headed down the hall toward his study, and turned his head to speak to her over his shoulder. "Fix us a meal they won't soon forget, Angel."

A moment later he began to whistle. When Jessica identified the tune, her fury burned even hotter. "The Old Gray Mare."

"Oooooooo, you are *such* a toad!" She screeched in his direction. With a defiant stomp of her foot she marched to her bedroom. Tabby appeared out of nowhere and sauntered across the doorway. She roared in a voice made him jump for safety. "Get out of my way, cat!"

In her room, she paced, muttering to herself. "Fix them a meal they won't forget." She addressed the wall that lay in the direction of his study. "Well, you can bet your stinkin' meatloaf on that, Jason Rawlings. Believe me, you can definitely count on that."

Thirteen

Jessica rose bright and early the following morning, her blood still boiling from the night before. He had made her the world's biggest fool, and during the night she'd hatched a plan to get even. She slammed the coffeepot under the kitchen faucet, spraying water all over herself and the cabinet in her haste. She had just plugged it in and reached for her coffee cup when she heard a noise behind her.

Jason asked, "Jessica, where did you put my clean underwear?"

"In your top drawer where I always do." She turned to face him, and her mouth dropped open. He stood in the doorway wearing nothing but a towel wrapped around his slender waist. Her face felt like a four-alarm fire.

"They're not there," he replied casually, as if nothing out of the ordinary was occurring. "I just looked."

Jessica stood frozen. She couldn't help but seeing his massive chest with the thick, soft curly hair, and had to force her eyes to fix on his face. Then with a whirl that made her dizzy, she presented her back to him and faced the kitchen window.

"What do you think you're doing?" she asked through clenched teeth.

"I think I'm looking for my clean underwear." The matter-of-fact tone grated on her nerves "Why?"

"You know very well why." Her voice came out in a yell. She swallowed against a dry throat, and lowered her tone. "You don't have one stitch of clothes on."

"Well, I just thought after that dress you had on last night, you had decided we didn't have to be quite so formal around the house anymore."

She detected a mocking smirk, but dared not turn around to see his expression. Instead, she slammed her coffee cup down on the cabinet. "I certainly wouldn't call wearing clothes being formal."

"Okay," he said. "Now that we've defined acceptable household attire, I'll go back to my dresser and check again. I could have overlooked them."

"You do that," she gritted out.

She followed his progress by the sounds of his bare feet scuffing the carpet.

Jessica had just poured her coffee, trying to steady her nerves, when his voice floated down the hall.

"Well, what do you know? They're right here where you said they were."

Jessica stepped out onto the back porch to shake a small area rug. The air held a hot, stifling stillness this morning. From the looks of the sky in the distance they might get rain by tonight.

But no storms, please, she prayed silently.

The storms that could sweep through this small Texas town had always terrified her. Although she'd never actually been in a tornado, she had heard some hair-raising tales from Uncle Fred and Aunt Rainey concerning ones they had experienced. As a child she'd listened, wide-eyed, and decided that she would happily forgo that experience.

Just as she finished shaking the rug, the mailman pulled up to the mailbox to deposit the mail. She waved at him as he drove on down the dusty road, and then gathered the handful of bills and advertisements from the big box. Tucked between the junk, she found a letter addressed to her. She smiled as she recognized the handwriting of old Mrs. Houseman, her landlady in Austin. Jessica had dropped her a short note when she moved into Jason's house, informing her that she would be staying on here. She'd supplied Jason's home phone number and address where she could be reached in case of an emergency.

Jessica ripped open the letter. Through the last few years, Mrs. Houseman had mothered her. If Jessica was sick, her elderly landlady would be the first to show up at her door with a jar of her homemade chicken soup and a big bottle of Dr. Caldwell's laxative. Mrs. Houseman held the opinion that Dr. Caldwell's was the answer to anyone's ills, no matter what the diagnosis.

Her eyes scanned the pastel paper, trying to read Mrs. Houseman's scratchy writing. "Don't worry about the lease, dear," she wrote. "There was a young girl by here this morning wanting to know if the apartment was available, and though I'll miss you something fierce, I know your place is at home right now. I'll be happy to pack your belongings and send them along to you."

Jessica's eyes teared up as she folded the letter back

up. Her plans to make Jason fall in love with her again were as far away as ever. For a moment, she toyed with the idea of moving back into Uncle Fred and Aunt Rainey's house at the end of this six month arrangement, but dismissed it. In all likelihood, she'd have to return home in Austin permanently. Unless things changed, she would never be able to live here in this town when she and Jason parted. She would never be able to live in the small town with him, seeing him married to Monica. No, she couldn't live through that. Instead of coming out of this "arrangement" unscathed, she had succeeded only in falling in love more deeply with Jason.

Jessica sighed. She would write Mrs. Houseman and ask her to hold the apartment for her. Her heart heavy, she returned to the house to do that.

As she entered the kitchen, phone shrilled. She jerked the phone off its cradle. She wasn't in the mood for a phone conversation this morning. "Hello!"

"Wow, I'm sorry," Maureen Winters's voice apologized. "The day this young and going so bad already?"

"Bad isn't the word," Jessica told her. "This whole week has been the pits."

"Well, old Dr. Winters has just the right prescription. Let's go out to lunch and do some shopping."

"I can't," Jessica responded, toying absently with a lock of hair. "Jason has invited Willis and Marcy over for dinner this evening. I have to do the shopping for that, and then come home and tear up the house."

"Tear up the house?" Maureen laughed. "Don't you mean clean up the house?"

Oops. She didn't intend to say that. "Uh, yeah. Listen, Maureen, I'm sorry, but I can't chat right now. Can I call you tomorrow?"

"Sure, no problem," Maureen said. "I'll talk to you then."

Jessica placed the receiver and gave it a threatening

look which forbade it to ring again. She hurried to the bathroom for a quick shower, then donned a pair of white slacks with a navy-blue top, applied a light coat of mascara to her lashes and a touch of gloss to her pink lips. She then twisted her thick hair into a knot, pinned it securely to the top of her head, and pulled free a few wispy tendrils to hang down the sides and back. Satisfied with her work, she picked up the keys to the Lincoln from the basket that was lying on the kitchen counter and let herself out the back door.

She cruised to the market slowly in the elegant luxury of Jason's air-conditioned car. Songs from her favorite CD, "Hooked on Classics," drifted from the elaborate stereo system She parked the Continental in front of Mr. Sweeney's store and jumped out onto the hot pavement. The cool air inside the store instantly dried the perspiration that had erupted during the short walk from the car to the building. Grabbing a cart, she started down the aisle, fighting the temptation to squeeze the Charmin as the old toilet paper commercial emerged from childhood memory.

At the meat counter, she selected the hamburger that looked as if it had the most suet in it. She wanted her meatloaf to be just right, with enough grease to float a battleship. Continuing down the aisle, she hand-picked the vegetables to go into the meatloaf. The green pepper was so limp and tough she would have to use the electric carving knife to chop it up. A cart of discarded lettuce sat next to the produce department— heads of brown wilted lettuce ready to be taken to the back to be dumped. She stopped her cart next to it and casually selected the sickest-looking head in the basket. With a smug smile, she plunked it into her cart.

When she came to the check-out stand, Mr. Sweeney greeted her warmly and started to remove the items from Jessica's cart. When he reached for the head of lettuce his face paled.

"Jessica, let me get you another head." He left his register and started for the produce counter.

"No, Mr. Sweeney, that one will do just fine."

He gave her a puzzled look. "But this was going to be thrown away. I'll get you a fresh, crisp head that we just unpacked. It won't take a minute."

"No." Jessica stood firm. "That's the one I want."

Mr. Sweeney looked helpless. Finally, he shrugged. "Well, I'm certainly not going to charge you for it." He finished ringing up the items in her cart.

Leaving the store feeling satisfied, Jessica drove home humming under her breath. "This will definitely be a meal they won't forget, Jason." she muttered.

At home, she unloaded her groceries and brought them in, setting the brown paper bags on the kitchen counter. After she put the perishables in the refrigerator and the canned goods in the cabinet, she tore around the living room disarranging throw pillows, draping various items of clothing over chairs, scattering newspapers haphazardly around.

She sprinkled a sack of popcorn on the floor and threw a couple of pairs of Jason's boots, covered with cow dung, next to his chair. She set several glasses full of ice on the end tables. It would be melted by the time the guests arrived. Standing back, she admired the mess she'd created. It would do. Now for the food.

She spent the rest of the afternoon working on the meal itself, not bothering to wash up any of the dishes after she used them. Instead, she left them sitting around on the cabinet to grow dry and crusty. The floor looked like it had snowed from all the flour she scattered around while mixing her cake. She had a great time, humming under her breath and working as hard as a beaver.

When Jason opened the door that evening, the house looked like the predicted approaching storm had already hit. She concealed herself behind the doorsill and peeked to see his reaction. His eyes widened in astonishment before he pulled a calm mask over his face.

He stepped into the room and called over his shoulder. "Come on in, Eric. Jessie must be in the kitchen."

Eric?

Jason's younger brother, Eric, followed him through the door, talking as he walked. "I can't wait to see her after all these years. I bet she'll be surprised. She doesn't know I'm here, does she?" Eric came to a halt, his eyes mirroring Jason surprise as he surveyed the living room.

Jessica jerked back into the safety of the kitchen and swallowed a groan. Why did he pick today to show up?

"Yes, I bet she will be surprised," Jason agreed. "I tried to call her this morning when I found out you were flying in, but I couldn't reach her."

Drat! She'd left her cell phone at home on the charger when she went to the store, and had been too busy to check it since she returned home.

"Well, I sure wish Rena could have made the trip, but Scottie had a summer cold, so she thought she had better stay home with him this time."

"Maybe the next trip."

She peeked around the corner in time to see Jason pitch the cat's bowl out of his chair. He motioned to Eric to take a seat.

"Jessie has changed things quite a bit." Jason stretched out in his chair. "You wouldn't recognize this old house."

Eric's reply sounded wary. "No, that's for sure."

Her shaky knees nearly dumped her on the floor. This was not turning out at all as she'd hoped.

Calm down. Eric always had a great sense of humor. Maybe he'll think it's funny as the evening progresses.

She shouted into the living room. "Are our guests

here yet, Jason?"

"Part of them, Angel. Come on out here. I've got a surprise for you."

Was that a snicker she heard in his voice?

Drawing a breath for strength, she stepped through the doorway and made of show of Jessica stopping dead in her tracks. "Eric?"

Eric jumped up from his chair, crossed the room, swooped her off her feet in a tremendous bear hug, and swung her around the room.

"My Lord, you're prettier than ever." His grin stretched from ear to ear.

Eric wasn't as tall as Jason, but he possessed the same golden-brown hair and luscious green eyes. He'd always been the biggest tease of all the boys and usually said the first thing that popped into his head, regardless of decorum.

"Why in the world would you want to get hooked up with this bum again?" He pointed at Jason and grinned broadly.

Jessica replied in a light tone. "Oh, we still hate each other. I'm only working for him now. It's strictly a 'business agreement'."

Jason gave her a big grin and a mock salute with his hand. "Touché."

"Well, if I had known you weren't too particular who you worked for, I would have been down here trying for you myself." Eric awarded her a saucy wink.

"What would Rena think about that?" Jason commented dryly.

Eric feigned innocence. "Rena who?"

"Rena who?" Jessica echoed.

"My adorable wife"—Eric grinned—"and she's a mean woman when she gets her hackles up."

Jessica gave him one big hug before letting go of his neck. "I am so happy to see you. I had no idea you would be here tonight." She shot Jason a dirty look.

"Didn't know I was coming myself until the last minute." Eric returned to the sofa. "I had some papers that needed Jason's signature, so I hopped a plane and flew down this afternoon."

"How have you been?" She tried unobtrusively to stuff a pair of Jason's dirty socks under the cushion of her chair.

"Can't complain." He leaned forward, his puzzled eyes roaming the cluttered room.

Jason pushed himself back up out of his chair. "Come on, Eric. You can wash up before dinner if you'd like. Just put your bags in your old room. You'll have to shove a couple of saddles out of the way." He turned to Jessica. "Eric's going to spend the night here and take the early flight out tomorrow morning."

"How...nice." Her heart sank. What would he think of the coming dinner?

Eric stood, picked up his suitcase, and followed Jason down the hall. "Your cat not trained?" He asked as his eyes took in all the newspapers lying on the floor.

"No, it's trained," she heard Jason's deep voice say as they reached his room. "Just put your things in there, and we'll let you know when dinner's ready."

The peal of the doorbell brought Jessica back to her feet, scurrying for the kitchen at a run.

"I'll get it, Angel," Jason called sweetly.

"Thank you, Jason," she responded in the same sweet tone as she slammed through the kitchen door.

Once again Jessica took up her post by the doorway and peeked.

"Ms. Vogue" and her "brown shoe" were smiling brightly as Jason opened the door and let them into the cluttered room. To Jessica's satisfaction, Marcy's eyebrow rose in distaste, but she recovered her composure. Willis was obviously just along for the ride. Judging by the expression on his face, all was as it should be.

"Jason, darling." Marcy clutched his arm. "How nice

of you to have us in your home!"

"I'm glad you could come this evening, Marcy, Willis. Come in and sit down. I think dinner's almost ready."

Marcy headed for a chair beside Jason's, but discovering the seat full of cookie crumbs, she moved to the sofa.

Willis sat down in the pile of cookie crumbs.

Jessica returned to her work putting the finishing touch on the 'special' dinner, but kept her ear tuned to the conversation in the living room. She could hear everything from the dining room.

"Could I get you both something to drink?" Jason sounded like the gentleman owner of a manner house, just like he wasn't sitting in the middle of a disaster.

"No, thank you," Willis replied. "I'm fine, really."

"Nothing for me, darling," Marcy piped up. "I still have to watch my figure, you know. I was telling Willis on the drive over here, just because I have children now doesn't mean I can let myself go. Most people are shocked when they find out I have children. Isn't that what I was telling you, sweetie?"

Jessica set a fifth plate on the table and pretended to gag herself with a finger.

Willis answered in the manner of a truly henpecked husband. "I told her she looks just fine to me, don't you think? I mean really fine?"

"Yes, she looks just fine." Jason repeated.

Jessica snickered. They sounded like a room full of parrots.

Time to make an appearance. Jessica came through the kitchen door. The men both stood, and Jason took her arm. "Everything going all right? Do you need any help in the kitchen?"

"No, I can handle things just fine, thank you." She turned a pleasant expression toward their guests and mimicked Jason's polite manners. "Good evening, Marcy. Willis."

"Good evening, Jessica," Willis said. "Jason certainly has a lovely home." He reached out to shake her hand. Jessica felt like she was squeezing a nerf ball. "It's just so homey-looking," he said sincerely.

Their eyes took in the disarray in the living room.

"Yes, that's what I told Jessie," Jason piped up. "Now, this is a room a man can really be at home in."

Jessica couldn't believe her ears. He was actually enjoying this.

Willis indulged in a habit that had always driven Jessica crazy—he sucked on his front teeth. That sucking, squeaky noise grated on her nerves. Many was the time when she could have cheerfully strangled him.

Jessica was never so relieved as to hear Eric's booming voice behind her.

"I don't know about anyone else, but I'm starving. I've had to put up with Jason's bragging all afternoon about what a great cook his—uh, housekeeper is. Now I'm ready to be convinced."

Jessica managed a weak smile. "Everything's ready now. We can eat anytime."

"Then, madam, if I may?" He held out his arm Jessica and led her into the dining room.

Jason escorted a chattering Marcy, with Willis trailing along behind, sucking on his teeth.

The table was lovely in its simplicity. A fresh bouquet of late-summer flowers nestled elegantly in a peanut-butter jar in the center of the table. She had placed gaily flower-patterned Melmac in front of each chair. Sparkling clean jelly glasses caught the light from the glittering chandelier, waiting to be filled with the cherry Kool-Aid Jessica had made to complement the meal. Two candle stubs in brass holders rested next to the flower centerpiece.

Jason seated Marcy and dramatically lit the candle stubs before Jessica brought in the food. "The table looks lovely, Jessie."

How do I get myself in these messes?

"Excuse me a moment and I'll get our dinner."

In the kitchen, she slammed pots and pans around with such force she was sure the people in the other room thought there was a war going on.

Eric thinks I'm an absolute basket case. Why did everything have to backfire on me like this?

But she was committed now. There was no turning back.

She began dishing up the vegetables and potatoes in all the mismatched bowls she could drag out of the cabinet. Defiantly she marched back to the dining room, slamming bowls down on the table, and returning for more.

The guests sat quietly, expressions on their faces ranging from mild surprise to deep puzzlement to outright astonishment. Jason's eyes, however, held only mild amusement.

Jessica shoved the large bowl of potatoes under Eric's nose and asked in a curt tone if he would mind passing them. Then she turned to Jason. "I'm bringing in the meatloaf now. Would you mind serving?"

"Of course not. Can hardly wait to taste it." He smiled at his guests. "Wait until you taste her meatloaf. You're in for the treat of your life."

Jessica fired him a disgusted look and returned to the kitchen. Moments later she returned with a meat platter bearing the nearly charred remains of the meatloaf.

She looked at the blank expressions on the four faces, and announced, "Jason prefers his meat well done."

To her surprise, he backed her up. "I don't like any pink left in my meat." He picked up a large carving knife and began slicing generous servings of tough, dry meatloaf for each plate. "Ahhhhh...just the way I like it." He looked up and smiled adoringly at her.

Eric picked up the bowl of potatoes and spooned some onto his plate, leaning down to peer closer at them. "Are these mashed or fried, Jessie?"

"Mashed," she replied curtly.

He passed the bowl on to Marcy, who, in turn, immediately passed it on to Willis.

"You know, Jessica excelled in home ec in high school," Jason said.

Marcy muttered under her breath, "You must be kidding."

As Jason picked up Marcy's plate to serve her meat she practically shouted, "Just a very small serving for me." She cleared her throat and cast an apologetic glance around the table. "I try not to eat too heavily in the evening."

"Oh, but you must let down just for tonight," Jessica urged.

The table was laden with a dazzling array of starches, all for Marcy's benefit. First Jessica passed a large bowl of corn, then one each of hominy and pork and beans, followed by a bowl of creamed peas so thick you could easily have hung wallpaper with them. The tossed salad looked like someone's garbage, and the Jell-O salad contained large chunks of pineapple floating in a not-quite-congealed green ooze.

Eric surveyed the table with awe. "You got enough starch here to start a Chinese laundry."

She flushed a bright red, and turned to Jason. "You haven't served Eric his meat, Jason."

"Oh, sorry." He grinned at his brother. "Pass your plate, bubby and take it like a man."

"Could I have some catsup, please?" Eric ducked his head in a half-apology. "I always eat my meatloaf with catsup."

"I'll get you some." Eric was being so pathetically obliging about eating his meal Jessica had a hard time keeping a straight face.

"Jessica," Willis said when she brought the catsup back to the table and set it before a grateful Eric, who was trying to work his way through the gooey peas, "this is a fine meal. Marcy is an excellent cook, but she rarely fixes so many—rib sticking dishes at one time." The banker gave her an angelic smile.

Jessica grabbed her napkin and covered her mouth before she let out a stifled giggle. Willis had little black pieces of burned meatloaf stuck between his teeth.

"Why, that's sweet of you, Willis, but I don't want to mislead you. I don't cook quite this heavy a meal for Jason every night—just on special occasions, like tonight."

Eric glanced up from his plate, started to say something, but apparently thought better of it. Instead he gave Jessica a devilish grin and turned regretfully back to his food. The grin did a lot to soothe her conscience. Maybe he'd caught on to her plan.

The ghastly meal finally came to an end. Everyone ate lightly except for Willis, who took seconds of everything.

Jason suggested they have their coffee and dessert in the living room. They all left the table with the zeal of refugees leaving a war zone.

Jessica brought the tray with coffee and cups in, placing it on the low table in front of the sofa. She left briefly, returning with the chocolate cake that had fallen in the middle when she iced it hot from the oven. Four sets of eyes immediately focused on everything in the room but the cake. Jessica had used so many toothpicks to hold the cake together it looked as if it had been shot with a pellet gun.

Jessica handed Marcy her coffee first.

"Oh, hot tea," Marcy remarked, looking at the almost clear liquid in the bottom of her cup. "How nice for a change."

"No," Jessica answered coolly, "it's coffee. Jason

can't sleep nights if I make it too strong."

Eric sat up straighter, peering into his cup. "Well, you ought to sleep like the dead tonight."

Willis started to squeak and suck on his teeth again. Jessica's nerves stretched nearly to the breaking point. Would this night ever end?

Jason shot Willis a dirty look. He reached over to the cake, withdrew a toothpick, and offered it to him silently.

They made small talk for another hour or so before Willis and Marcy said their good-byes, and Eric retired to his room early.

Jason saw the Mercys to the front door, closed and locked it behind them. He switched off the large yard light and turned back to Jessica, who still sat in the devastated living room.

He crossed the room and stood beside her chair.

"Thank you for an outstanding meal tonight. Truly unforgettable."

Her mouth gaped open while her mind conducted a frantic search for a response.

He started toward his bedroom, whistling "Auld Lang Syne."

Jessica's eyes fell on the hideous chocolate cake. The horrendous thing blurred as tears welled up in her eyes. She had tried so hard to take revenge on him for refusing her advances last night, but he'd turned the tables on her. Instead of being angry or embarrassed, he acted like a complete gentleman. Laying her head on her arm, she released the pent-up tears and sobbed her heart out.

When her tears subsided, and she made her way down the hall to her bedroom. This plan had gone down the drain along with the others.

Fourteen

A violent clap of thunder jerked Jessica out of a sound sleep. Outside the wind roared. The limbs of the old tree by her bedroom window made grotesque patterns on the wall in her room, against the security light left burning all night in the farmyard.

She raised up on her knees to peer through the window just as a jagged streak of lightning forked through the sky, followed by a deafening boom which shook the entire house. Heart pounding, she scurried to the foot of her bed. The rain had not started yet. It seemed to be one of the violent electrical storms that came up occasionally. The kind she hated the most.

Another lightning bolt shot across the sky. When she was small, she would always run into Uncle Fred and Aunt Rainey's room, crawl between them, and bury her head under the covers. Aunt Rainey would pull her close, pat her back, and tell her not to be afraid. "It's just the angels' potato wagons falling over," she'd say comfortingly. Then another deafening clap would come, and Jessica would say, "They sure must have big potatoes."

Oh, how she longed for those comforting arms tonight!

Another peek through the window showed the wind whipping the branches of the old oak violently now. The streaks of lightning were following almost on top of one another, with the thunder sounding like sonic booms.

Calm down, Jessica. You're a big girl now. No need to be afraid.

But she was. Cringing, she pulled the curtain shut across the window in an ineffective attempt to block out the raging storm.

She pulled the pillow up over her ears, but even that didn't muffle the sound. Above her head, the wind rattled the window, and she shivered in terror. What if it broke? She needed to get away, to someplace safer. But where? The bathroom, maybe? That was an interior room, with no windows and sturdy walls reinforced by plumbing. Yes, the bathroom.

She crawled out of bed, dragging her quilt with her. Wrapping the blanket tight around her shoulders, she hurried to the door and threw it open as another blast of thunder exploded. With a screech, she dashed into the hallway—

And straight into Jason.

"What are you doing in here?" she asked.

"I woke up and happened to remember a little violet-eyed pixie who has an unnatural fear of storms." He enfolded her in his arms. "I thought she need some reassurance about now."

The deafening boom of another loud clap of thunder

shook the house again, and buried her face tightly in his neck.

"C'mon, Angel."

He guided her to the living room, dropped on the sofa, and pulled her down beside him. With an arm around her shoulders, he pulled her tightly, securely against him. Though she remained wrapped in the quilt, his body felt wonderfully warm.

"How did you know I was afraid of storms?"

"I was there one day when you came running in Rainey's back door during a spring thunderstorm, your face as white as a sheet." The memory stirred up a tender chuckle, which she felt in his chest.

"I know it's silly." She sighed. "And it's something I've tried to overcome, but I'm still deathly afraid of storms."

"It's all right," he whispered as the storm raged on in its full fury. "It's the angels' potato wagons falling over?' He teased. "Besides, how many times lately have I had to hold beautiful woman in my arms?"

A woman's arms. He finally thought of her as a woman, and a beautiful one.

Outside, the rain began. Huge drops pelted hard against the windows as she snuggled closer to him, her head fitting smoothly into the curve where his arm met his chest.

"Why are you so special?" He was so uniquely...hers.

His mouth opened in a huge yawn, and then he shifted his position sideways so he could lean against the sofa's padded arm, pulling her with him. "I don't know what I'm going to do with you, Angel, but I'm too tired to figure it out tonight. Go to sleep."

And she did— as rain pelted the old farmhouse, she slept peacefully, calmly, and most contentedly in his arms.

❦

Rain was still falling softly when she felt Jason heave himself off the couch. She mumbled a protest, and cracked open an eye.

"What are you doing up so early?" she whispered. "It's hours before daybreak."

"Shhh." A warm finger laid across her lips. "Go back to sleep. I've got a couple of farms to run."

She snuggled deeper into the couch cushion to enjoy another few hours of sleep before she faced the new day. As she drifted back to sleep she heard him and two of his farmhands slam the doors of their trucks, start their motors, and drive out of the farmyard.

The next sound she heard was that of Eric's electric razor in the hall bathroom. She lay there in lazy limbo for a few minutes, thinking of the night before, and poor Eric's face through the whole nightmarish part of the evening. A soft giggle escaped. What must be going through his mind this morning? The pigsty of a house, the horrendous meal.

She jumped off the couch and dashed to her room to pull on a pair of old jeans and a soft yellow cotton T-shirt. Picking up her hairbrush, she brushed rapidly through the tangled mess until it crackled in the early morning air. Then she hurried to the kitchen.

The smell of coffee perking and ham frying in the large iron skillet on the stove filled the kitchen as Eric entered a little later.

"Good morning, pretty lady," he said cheerfully. "What's got you out of bed so early on a dreary morning like this?"

"Good morning to you." She filled her voice with the affection she had for Jason's younger brother. "How about some breakfast?"

His face paled slightly before he pleaded, "Just coffee, please. My stomach is a little queasy this morning."

"Nonsense." Jessica smiled. "I owe you a decent

breakfast after what I put you through last night. Sit down. I promise you your meal will be different this morning."

He let out a long breath as he pulled out the chair at the kitchen table and settled his long frame in it. "I got to tell you, Jessie, that meal hung heavy on my stomach all night. I'm afraid I've cleaned you out of Alka-Seltzer."

Jessica giggled as she placed a mug of hot coffee before him. He sat up straighter and peered intently into his cup as if to assure himself it wasn't of the same quality as the previous night's. Apparently satisfied, he picked up the cream pitcher and added a liberal portion to the strong black liquid. Jessica turned back to the counter, preparing to mix batter for hot cakes. She set the large cast-iron griddle on the burner to heat, then began mixing up the batter.

"How long have you and Rena been married?"

"Three years last month. You would really like her, Jessie. She's the best-looking blonde you've ever laid eyes on, believe me."

Jessica smiled as she picked up a wooden spoon and began beating the thick batter in a rapid motion. "You wouldn't be just a little partial, now, would you, Eric?"

He picked up his coffee cup and he took another sip of his coffee before conceding, "Maybe a little. But that doesn't mean it isn't true."

Jessica chuckled as she spooned out the batter onto the sizzling hot grill. The hotcakes puffed up slightly before bubbling on top. She flipped over the golden-brown cakes, which gave off a mouth-watering aroma. Removing the first two cakes, she generously spread them with golden butter and handed the plate to Eric before spooning more onto the hot griddle.

"How old is your little boy?" she asked.

Eric had a bottle of maple syrup in his hand and

was drowning his cakes in the gooey, sweet liquid. "He's a year and a half." He flashed a wide grin and laid his fork down. A moment later he produced a cell phone that had at least fifty pictures of a smiling, chubby, blond-haired boy.

Jessica's eyes misted as she looked at the beautiful child, who bore a strong resemblance to his father and uncle. *Is this what Jason's baby would look like?* She scanned the pictures, seeing the chubby baby go from an infant to an endearing toddler. Would she ever have the honor of carrying Jason's children, seeing the proud look on his face that was now radiating from Eric's? The last picture was of a very lovely blond woman holding the baby, her eyes shining with a mother's love. She wore the look of a very contented woman, one who had found her place in life with her child and her husband.

"This must be Rena," Jessica said softly. Pangs of envy shot through her as she gazed at the picture of this woman who seemed to have everything important in life.

"That's her." His love for Rena waved in his face like a red banner.

"She's very beautiful," Jessica assured him, "and Scottie's a real angel."

"Kids are great. We want at least six." He returned to his hot cakes. "What about you and old Jase—you thinking of gettin' married again? He isn't getting any younger, you know."

Jessica was removing the last hot cake from the grill as she felt the tears welling up in her eyes. They started running down her cheeks faster than she could wipe them away.

Eric looked up with surprise, his expression turning to a worried frown as he saw the river rolling down her face. "Did I say something wrong, honey?" Grabbing a napkin from the table, he began awkwardly mopping at her tears. "Sit down, Jessie." He pulled her over to the table and placed her in the chair across from his, still wiping ineffectually at her tears.

She felt like a total basket case now, the flood gates of the dam completely opened.

"Jessica!" A note of panic sounded in his voice. "Will you please tell me what in the world's going on. I feel like I've stayed overnight at the zoo—in the monkey cage."

"Oh, Eric, I'm so miserable," she sobbed, "and I'm making Jason miserable. Everything is in a miserable mess." Her slim shoulders shook violently as she sat at the table, ready to pour her heart out to the one man she hoped could tell her what to do.

"What are you talking about? Are you and Jason having a little quarrel? Good heavens, that's nothing to get so upset over. Rena and I average one a day, but that doesn't mean I don't love her."

"Oh, Eric, you just d— d—don't understand. Jason doesn't love me, period. The only reason we're together at all is this stupid business arrangement. I'm paying him thirty thousand dollars to stay here and run my farm for me until November, when I can collect my inheritance." She stopped to blow her nose. Her face felt hot, the skin puffy from all the crying. "Uncle Fred and Aunt Rainey stipulated in their will that I had to come home and run the farm for six months or all my inheritance would go elsewhere. At first, I didn't care, but then I know how hard my aunt and uncle worked to build this farm, and I can invest the inheritance in my business in Austin, so I offered Jason the opportunity to make extra money if he would help me out." She blew her nose again loudly. "He agreed to the arrangement, I guess, partly because he felt sorry for me, partly because he needed the money."

"*Needed* the money?" Eric interrupted. "Jessica, this is getting crazier by the minute."

Jessica sniffed hard, then looked up at Eric. "What do you mean?"

"Hasn't Jason told you anything about his finances?" His expression was openly incredulous.

"Of course not. We don't talk about that sort of thing."

Eric reached up and ran his fingers through his thick hair, clearly disturbed by this mind-boggling conversation. "Jessica, it's not my place to tell you Jason's business, but you two should stop fighting and sit down and have a long talk. I can't believe he's never told you anything about his life after you left."

"Why should he?" she hiccupped. "I'm nothing to him but a business arrangement."

"You mean to sit there and tell me that my brother, Jason, who is the most level-headed one in this whole family, is just doing this for you as a favor? Sorry—for thirty thousand dollars?" Eric shook his head, eyeing her with pity. "Then he's going to up and walk out on you in November? Go his own separate way? Honestly, do you think you can make me believe that? That's a heckuva of a lot of hard work for Jason."

Clearly, he didn't believe a word she was saying, and that was starting to irritate her. "Well, it's the truth, whether you believe it or not."

"Then you've missed your calling," he said. "You should be selling ocean-front property in Kansas."

She laid her head on the table and gave in to desperation. "Oh, Eric, what am I going to do? I love him more than anything in the world."

He shook his head in disbelief as he got up to pour himself and Jessica more coffee. "Wish I could tell you, honey, but I can't make heads nor tails out of any of this." Suddenly his eyes softened. "You really love the guy, don't you? You know what? I've always known you loved him, since you were a child. It was always there, plain as the nose on your face."

"I love him more than life itself, but I've lost him forever." A return of the sobs threatened. "He can't forgive me for letting the annulment take place."

He laid a steadying hand on her shoulder. "I think you're borrowing trouble. Jason doesn't take his personal affairs lightly. Who knows, he could still be in love with you. Something must have caused him to agree to this arrangement of your."

"There is," she nodded, miserable. "Money. Oh, how I wish I could undo the past, but I can't. Now he's involved with a woman named Monica, and I don't know—he may be in love with her. She certainly is with him. And who can blame her? He's...perfect in every way."

"Jessica," Eric said kindly, "did you ever stop to think that not everyone sees him through your eyes? Jason's just an average guy, no better, no worse than the next guy. You're looking at him through the eyes of love, honey."

"What do you mean?" she snapped. "He's wonderful."

"If you say so." He paused. "I mean, I guess he is—he's really not my type. But what I'm trying to say is you've got to take him down off that pedestal you've had him on all these years. You're just as lovely a woman as he is a man. If you want him, go after him."

"I've tried, truly I have. Just the other night—" She bit her lip. No need to embarrass herself further by describing her disastrous attempt to make him notice her as a woman. Then she looked at the expression on Eric's face, and a sprig of hope bloomed in her heart. "Do you really think I would stand a chance with him again?"

"I don't know, but I can tell you this. I think I know my brother well, and I have never—I repeat, never—known him to do anything unless he knew exactly what he was doing." He picked up his fork and tackled his hotcakes. "I have a strong hunch that things are not nearly as dark as you picture them."

After Eric left to catch his plane, Jessica poured her fourth cup of coffee. Her mind replayed their conversation over and over. Would she really ever have a chance to become Jason's wife again? Was she looking at him only through the eyes of love? How could she ever look at him any other way? She didn't know—all she knew was she did love him. And it hurt.

Fifteen

The weeks crawled by. The intense heat of summer blended slowly into fall. The six-month "business arrangement" crept steadily toward an end as October opened its arms to the world.

To Jessica's dismay, Jason seemed more grimly determined than ever to keep his distance. After one or two more subtle attempts to capture his attention romantically, she scratched that plan. Every time she tried, his mocking eyes openly laughed at her. That man was a tough bird—one that couldn't be led down the garden path easily.

Late one afternoon, Jessica sat in a chair in the kitchen lovingly stroking a very pregnant Tabby, who had been renamed Tabacina when evidence of her condition proved that someone had made a grave error in gender determination. Lethargy dragged at Jessica's limbs. The stress of living under the same roof with the man she loved, and the pain of knowing she could never have him, was taking a toll. She was tired.

Jason came through the kitchen on his way to pick up Monica for their date that evening. She glanced up and her heart twisted in her chest. He looked tired too. In the last few weeks he'd taken very little time for his personal life. He left for work before sunup and returned long past sundown. The effort of keeping the two farms running efficiently must be exhausting. No matter how he had teased about the way he was going to spend his thirty thousand dollars, he must really be in financial need to put himself through all this misery. A wave of tenderness swept through her. She could manage to slip an extra thousand in his pay envelope when this job was over. The new children's line wasn't quite ready to launch; money wasn't a problem. An extra thousand would undoubtedly come in handy for a struggling farmer.

He stopped and knelt beside her. His clean smell washed over her, causing a tight knot to form in her throat. She closed her eyes momentarily fighting the urge to throw herself into his arms.

"How's the expectant mama coming along?" He asked lightly, running his large hand smoothly over Tabacina's soft fur.

Envy stabbed at her as she watched Jason's strong hand tenderly stroking the cat. How she longed for the gentle touch of those hands.

"Glowing," she said, striving to keep her voice steady. "I've warned her that's what happens to 'loose' women."

Jason chuckled softly and gave Tabacina one final pat before rising. "Now, what would you know about 'loose' women?"

"Not much," she admitted, and then grinned. "Tabacina could probably curl my hair with some of her wild experiences."

He leaned back against the counter, crossing his muscular arms. "When's the big event?"

"Huh?"

His forehead dipped toward the cat. "When are the kittens due?"

"Oh. Very soon—I think. I'm not too sure when her night of passion took place." She chuckled, and heat threatened to creep up her neck.

He ducked his head and forced her to meet his gaze. Jessica's heart thudded. Finally, he spoke in a quiet, serious tone. "I used to lie awake nights for the first few months after the annulment wondering if anything had ever come from that one 'night of passion' we spent together."

Her pulse kicked into high speed. "Come out of it? What do you mean?"

Jason continued to hold her gaze. "I wondered if maybe you were carrying my baby."

Emotions launched a battle in her. What did he take her for, someone who would deny her child his father? No, if that had happened—and she was heartbroken it hadn't—she would have told the world to go to Hades and been back in Jason's arms so fast it would have made everyone's head swim. Equally as strong as her indignation, pain throbbed in her chest. Did he really think she wouldn't have informed him about such an event?

This conversation had become far too intense. She was too tired, her feelings too raw, to have such a serious talk right now.

She sent Tabacina gently in her box and then faced Jason. Assuming a mock-serious voice, she said, "Jason, I really don't know how to tell you this." She paused effectively before continuing in dead earnest. "I have good news, and bad news."

Jason straightened, his arms falling to his sides and caution written all over his face. "What's the good news?"

"Weeeelllll," she said, dragging out the announcement with agonizing suspense, "I was pregnant with your child—in fact I had quadruplets."

Horror crept over his face. "Four babies?!" he choked out.

Jessica nodded.

With a visible effort, he managed to get himself under control. "What's the bad news?"

Assuming the attitude of extreme shame, she hung her head. "I gave all four of them away as Christmas presents."

Jason let out an exasperated snort. "Doggone it. Jessica, that's not funny."

There! That look of consternation on his handsome face was far more to her liking than the serious tone of a moment before. She let out a series of bubbly giggles. After a moment, a sheepish grin twisted his lips, and he took a playful swat at her shoulder. Jessica dodged his hand and dashed around the chair, placing it between them.

Still laughing, he dashed sideways, and she compensated by going the other way. They played a game of cat-and-mouse for a moment, both laughing like children.

Finally, he threw his hands up in defeat. "I'll make you pay for that."

Jessica's laughter caught in her throat. "I'm not afraid," she taunted, and cocked her head. "Do your worst, Rawlings."

A loud knock on the back door echoed through the room.

With a mock scowl at her, Jason yanked open the

back screen. A smiling Rick stood there, a bouquet of autumn flowers grasped in his hand. "Hi, boss. Where's the pretty lady?"

Jason jerked his head brusquely toward Jessica, still standing breathless in front of Tabacina's box. He brushed rudely past Rick and walked out the back door.

To his date with Monica. Her heart sank as she watched him go.

Rick threw a hesitant glance over his shoulder. "Have I come at a bad time?"

"No, of course not. What can I do for you?" Jessica forced her attention on the young man in front of her.

"These are for you, pretty lady." He extended the bouquet of flowers proudly.

She took them and automatically did what every woman does when receiving a bouquet of flowers—buried her nose in them. Not the sweet scent of spring blossoms, but these smelled of fresh air and rich soil and fragrant grasses. "They're beautiful, Rick. Thank you."

"There's a catch to them." He grinned broadly.

She couldn't help but return the smile. "And what might that be?"

"You have to agree to be my date for the hayride Saturday night."

"What hayride?" Jessica frowned.

"The one Jason has every fall. Hasn't he said anything about it to you?"

A vague memory surfaced. "It seems he did mention it awhile back. Is it this Saturday night?"

"Sure is. Every couple in love, engaged, or just 'hoping' will be there." His expression turned hopeful. "What do ya say? Will you go with me?"

Jason would undoubtedly be taking Monica. What else would she do, sit at home? "I'd love to."

She turned to find a vase for the flowers, but was interrupted when Rick scooped her up in his arms and whirled her around the room.

"Fantastic!" he shouted.

She offered him a glass of tea, and they spent a pleasant fifteen minutes in friendly chatter. Then he left to finish his chores.

Jessica waved good-bye, then closed the back door and leaned against its hard surface wearily. Her mind drifted lazily over the conversation with Jason, and their playful game of chase. That Jason, the lighthearted one, put in an appearance every so often. Whenever he did, she fell even more deeply in love with him. The torture of being around him every day, yet so far away, was becoming unbearable. She couldn't go on much longer. Soon she would have to throw in the towel, but her stubborn loving heart just wouldn't let her do it—yet.

The week flew by with the farm crew preparing for the hayride Saturday night. The big wagon was hauled up to the farmyard, and covered with bales of hay. One of the large farm tractors was attached to it and stood ready and waiting for the happy couples. According to Rick, the wagon would go about five miles down the road, where a barbecue dinner awaited them. Jason hired several people to cook for the boisterous group. Apparently, Monica had helped him plan this year's affair. Jessica tried not to feel hurt that he'd barely mentioned it to her.

He had asked her if she was going with Rick, and when she confirmed she was, he turned and left the room in a dark mood. She sighed deeply. If Jason had asked her, she would have said yes. But of course, he hadn't. No doubt who'd be at his side Saturday night, and it wouldn't be her.

She finished her chores as quickly as possible Saturday afternoon so she could be the first one in the shower this evening. The old relic of a hot-water heater had caused some trouble lately, providing only enough hot water for one person and leaving the other to shower rapidly in a stream of ice-cold water. With a triumphant smile, she barely managed to scurry past Jason that evening as he headed for the bathroom. Smiling pertly, she moved to close the door. "Sorry. I was here first!"

Jason stepped back slightly, eyes narrowed. "Couldn't you have showered earlier?"

"I've been busy, too." She tried unsuccessfully to close the door in his face.

He stuck out a hand, effectively blocking her move, a mischievous twinkle invading his eyes. "You use all that hot water, and you're a dead woman."

Jessica widened her eyes, and then blinked. "Would I do a thing like that to you?"

"You have three times this week already," he answered dryly.

"Tough luck, Rawlings." She threw her slight weight against the door.

Unfortunately, he held his ground, his muscled arms easily blocking her attempt. "You fool with me, and I'll turn off the hot water in the middle of your shower, Cole." It was Jason's turn to smile triumphantly.

She mulled over his threat. Would he follow through? Maybe, but probably not. He was a tease, but surely he wouldn't be that mean. He was just heckling her. Well, she could dish it out too.

Sighing dramatically, she batted her eyelashes. "I think a nice cold shower is just what I need. I feel it will help me control myself around Rick tonight. You know how romantic hayrides can be."

He gave her a disgusted look. She seized the advantage and slammed the bathroom door loudly in his face. Giggling impishly, she stripped her clothes off and left them in a heap on the floor as she turned the shower knobs on full blast and hopped in. The hot water soothed her tired body. Humming softly, she closed her eyes while steam from the hot water filled the room.

She'd just lathered her thick hair when the water changed from hot to ice-cold.

He did it! He actually did it!

"Jason, you dog!" she screamed at the top of her lungs.

From the other side of the bathroom door he shouted, "Just thought I'd help ole Rick out, Angel. I know how passionate you can get."

She finished her cold shower in a fit of anger and blazed out of the bathroom, still boiling. Jason was nowhere to be seen. She tracked into her room and slammed the door, jarring windows throughout the house.

She applied her makeup and then slipped on a pair of Fancy Duds designer jeans and a soft yellow top. A sound reached her—water running in the shower again. Throwing down her hairbrush, she rushed into the utility room and eyed the hot water heater. She had no idea how to turn it off. Instead, she took a large pail down from the top shelf, and filled it with cold water. In the kitchen, she dumped three trays of ice into the pail and tiptoed back down the hall. The water in the pail sloshed over the rim.

She stopped in front of the bathroom door and turned the doorknob slowly, hardly believing her luck. The dummy had left the door unlocked. Creeping stealthily into the bathroom, she stopped just outside the shower door and listened to Jason singing a boisterous version of "Blow the Man Down," totally unaware of his impending doom.

Moving as quietly as she could, Jessica raised the heavy pail over her head. Then, with a screeching karate cry, she dumped the icy contents over the shower curtain. Caught by surprise, the last note of Jason's song to sounded like the mating call of a banshee. When he issued a loud bellow of rage, she tossed the bucket aside and ran for her life.

She dashed down the hallway toward the kitchen, intent on escaping the house where, with luck, the farm hands were readying the hay wagon. He wouldn't pursue her there.

But she'd forgotten how fast he was. She'd barely made the living room when her wrist was grabbed by a soapy hand and she was roughly whirled around to face him. Still covered in suds, his thick hair white with lather, his eyes bulged. At least he'd taken the time to wrap a towel around his middle.

"Let me go." She twisted her wrist, but his grip held.

"Not a chance, Angel. You're going to pay for that."

He dragged her toward the kitchen, with her screeching at the top of her lungs. When they reached the counter, he put a wet arm around her middle to hold her in place, and with his other hand turned on the cold water.

"No! What are you going to do?"

"Give you a taste of your own medicine," he responded, a wicked laugh in the words.

The laugh brought an answering one of her own, only hers held an edge of playful outrage. "But that's what I just did to you. You started it."

She struggled, but could not free herself. Then he placed his hand on the back of her head and shoved her forward.

"Stop it." A scream ripped from her throat, but it sounded more like a laugh than anything. "I'm already dressed, you toad."

In the next instant, she sputtered as cold water hit the back of her head and splattered down her neck. Rivers ran down her face—her makeup would be ruined!—and saturated her hair. She let out another ear-piercing scream.

A loud pounding on the door shattered their mini-war. They both stopped struggling, and Jason released her.

"Who is it?" he shouted.

"Jason? What in the *world* is going on in there?" Monica's agitated voice reached them a moment before she opened the screen door.

Monica entered the kitchen and stopped dead in her tracks, her eyes going wide. For a moment, no one moved. Jessica stood there, rivers of water streaming from her hair down her face, gathering makeup along the way. Her shirt was soaked, and clung to her skin.

But Jason—

She glanced sideways. There he stood wearing nothing but a towel, covered in soap suds, his mouth gaping like a large-mouthed bass.

Jessica broke the tableau. She turned off the water.

Monica folded her arms across her chest. "What in heaven's name is going on here?"

Jason looked her directly in the eye, his face as innocent as a cherub. "What are you talking about?"

Monica's jaw dropped. "What am I *talking* about? I heard screams halfway across the front pasture. And there you stand wearing..." Her hand gestured, and her face flushed crimson. "And there *she* stands, drenched to the core...."

"Oh, that." He shrugged his broad shoulders, seemingly completely at ease, as if he weren't standing there nearly naked in front of the two women who loved him. "Jessica splashed dish soap in her eye, and apparently it stung. I heard her scream and I came running to help. I had to... flush it out."

Jessica turned a sideways look on him. Monica was no dummy. Surely she'd notice there was no soapy dishwater in the sink.

His brow arched as if to say, "Are we through? "Now, if you ladies will excuse me, I need to finish my shower."

He made a hasty exit, leaving a dissatisfied Monica

staring daggers at his back. When he was out of sight, she turned her glare on Jessica.

No way in the world I'm getting into this lover's spat.

Smiling, Jessica gestured toward the refrigerator. "Help yourself to lemonade. I need to get dressed...dry my hair...put on make-up." She glanced at the puddles of standing water littering the floor. "I'll take care of that later."

She left the kitchen at a near-run.

Sixteen

"Jessica, I need you here." Barb wailed on the other end of the phone. "Macy's is threatening to cancel their order if we don't meet with them next week. The place is falling apart without you."

Jessica propped the phone on a shoulder and applied her makeup with her free hand. "They're bluffing. They want a discount on their next order. We can afford to give it to them, can't we?"

"Well...yeah." Barb's voice held a world of reluctance. "But if we do that, Dillard's will be next. And when the rest of our retailers catch wind—"

Jessica cut her off. "Don't worry about it. I'll give Macy's a call tomorrow. Everything will work out, you'll see."

A brief pause sounded on the line. "We need you, Jessie. Everything is harder without you here."

Clutching the phone to her ear, Jessica gazed at the timer that told her she had less than two minutes before her baked beans needed to come out of the oven.

"I understand," she told Barb. "I'll try to arrange a flight next week. We'll work it out, okay?"

Relief sounded in her partner's voice. "Okay. Thanks, Jess. I can't wait to have you back here, where you belong."

The words rang in Jessica's mind long after she ended the call. Just where did she belong?

The hayride kicked off to a roaring start with everyone in high spirits. Close to thirty couples showed up, Willis and Marcy among them. Jessica had to smother a laugh when she first saw Willis. His new jeans—obviously bought off the rack—bagged unmercifully, his western shirt was outrageously loud, and his new Stetson resembled Quick Draw McGraw's. He was about as exciting as a cello player at a rock concert. Still, Jessica greeted him warmly and, almost against her will, caught his enthusiasm.

The night flew by with laughter and high spirits sweeping through the crowd. Toward the end of the evening, couples trailed off two-by-two, disappearing into the privacy of the darkened farm. Though Rick had been at his most charming all evening, Jessica felt absolutely zero attraction to him. He tried to beguile her with his lures, but in the end, she politely and firmly let him know she had no interest in his lighthearted foolishness.

All night long, everywhere she looked, Jason hovered nearby. If she seemed to be enjoying herself in

Rick's company, his deep scowl dampened her enthusiasm. Once Rick tickled her fancy with an amusing comment, and she let loose with a peal of laughter. Jason stopped his conversation with the driver of the hay wagon to jerk his head around and shoot her an irritated glance.

The huge barbecue, the horseshoe tournament, and sack race could have been loads of fun without his glowering presence. The rolling pin contest, in which the contestant who threw a rolling pin the farthest—indicating bad news for the boyfriend or spouse—won the prize, might have been the night's highlight. A red-faced Marcy Mercy took the trophy home while a grinning Willis, his hands jammed in his jean pockets, quietly beamed on the sidelines.

It was very late when everyone piled back on the wagon for the return trip home. Silence fell on the partiers as the moon crept higher in the sky. Couples found intimacy by wrapping in each other's arms. A man with a beautiful voice perched on a bale of hay and sang the sweet strains of "Moonlight Bay."

Rick tried to pull Jessica into his arms, but when she stiffened, maintained a respectful distance. She didn't want to encourage anything romantic with him, no matter how hard she teased Jason about him. He was a friendly, happy person to be with, but like all his predecessors, he left her feeling empty.

There was only one person she loved.

She shifted around on the hay, turning over to lie on her side more comfortably. Her breath froze as her gaze locked with Jason's. He was beside them on the hay, sitting close to Monica, who snuggled contentedly against his shoulder.

Electrical currents surged through her body as she began to slowly drown in the liquid fire of his beautiful jade eyes. Though she lay in another man's embrace, her breath became shallow, and she fought an overwhelming urge to reach out and grab Jason's hand.

Like a bolt of lightning, a thought occurred to her. She had reached her breaking point. No amount of money on earth could make her stay on here, dying a little more each day. Without the hope of a life with Jason, what was the use of staying?

The moment dawned with crystal clarity. She knew what she had to do.

Tears blurred her vision like a soft summer rain. Who cared about the children's clothing line Fancy Duds wanted to launch? She would, as she first intended, give Fred and Rainey's entire inheritance to the church. Rainey was a woman. She would understand that unresolved love demanded too high a price. Either she and Barb would find another funding source for the new children's line, or they would give up that dream. She couldn't do this anymore. Her only alternative was to give up the inheritance, go back to Austin, and try once more to fit the shambles of her life back together.

Completely unaware of the decision she'd just reached, Jason's emerald eyes drew her toward him. But he lay in another's embrace, as did she. This one last night she could allow herself to drown in his eyes, but it was all a sham. He would never belong to her again. She now belonged to Fancy Duds, and Austin, and the life she had ignored for the past several months.

Long after midnight, the hay wagon deposited the weary couples in the farmyard between Justin's house and the barn. Jessica climbed down, emotionally exhausted, longing only to reach the privacy of her room where she could cry her heart out alone.

Rick insisted on walking her to the door. As though he sensed the change in her mood, he pulled her into the comfort of his arms and gave her a reassuring hug. "I don't know what the problem is, pretty lady, but I pray things will look different in the morning."

She gave a shaky laugh. "I doubt it."

"Would you like to talk about it?"

His tone held nothing but understanding, acceptance, and comfort. Guilt shafted through her. She well knew he wanted more from her, but her heart belonged to another.

"No, thank you, Rick. It's something I have to work out alone."

He held her gaze in his. "Anytime you need someone, Jessica, I'll be here."

Oh, how she wished she could fall in love with him. If only she could take a surgical knife and cut all the painful memories and the love she had for Jason out of her heart.

Instead, she gave Rick a sisterly peck on the cheek and told him good night at the door.

Jessica sat wearily in her bedroom, fighting to make her mind a total blank, trying to erase the memories of the night. She brushed the loose hay out of her hair and took a quick shower—totally hot—before slipping into her nightgown. Her mind determined to imprison her as her thoughts once again drifted back to Jason's eyes. They'd held hers captive tonight. Her gaze fell on the pieces of hay scattered on her dressing table, and the dam of self-control finally broke. She switched off the light and fell across the bed, burying her face in the pillow and allowed the hateful tears to overcome her once more.

A loud bang as the door to her bedroom was thrown violently open brought her abruptly to her feet, the hot tears still streaming down her face. Jason stood in the doorway, still dressed in his hayride garb, his large frame blocking the light from the hall. He stood perfectly still, his eyes pits of deepest black.

"Are you in love with Rick?" The question sounded more like a demand.

Taken aback, Jessica couldn't think of an answer.

Steel shot through her backbone, and she asked, "Why does it matter to you?"

"Why?" The shadow of his frame seemed to grow. "Because you're driving me out of my mind!"

Heart pounding, Jessica remained silent. Neither moved. Finally, when the sounds of the night blared loud, Jason spoke. "Do you know what you put me through out there tonight on that hay wagon?"

The torture in his eyes, barely visible in the dim light, caused dual emotions to leap to the fore in Jessica. She closed her eyes, not daring to hope for the better of the two. "I didn't mean to. You're the one who started it."

"I...can't stand to sit there and watch you in some other man's arms."

A deep sigh escaped her lips. With an honesty that frightened her, she confessed, "I imagined I was in your arms."

"But you weren't, Angel." His whisper held a touch of torture. "How did we get ourselves in this mess?"

So many emotions warred in her, Jessica was afraid to answer. Given a word of encouragement, she would launch herself across the room and into his arms. But how could she even consider that? It was wrong, on so many levels.

Now is the time. I have to tell him.

"Jason," she whispered quietly.

He didn't answer, but his back stiffened slightly as he waited for her to go on.

"I'm going home—back to Austin—in the morning."

Emotions warred on his face. "Why?"

She closed her eyes, willing herself to deceive him. "My business needs me for a couple of important meetings this week. Plus, I need to check on my apartment. There are so many things I've been putting off."

And I need to get away from you, her heart cried.

Jason closed his eyes again, weariness etched

deeply in his tanned face. "That shouldn't take very long, should it?"

"I haven't decided how long; we're about to wind up most of the business matters, aren't we? The only thing left is the house, and it should sell soon." The admission stung like fire. The old house was falling apart but she had reservations about selling the place. Those would be set to rest once she stepped inside and saw the condition the bunk hands left once they moved out.

He shifted on his feet, his expression unreadable in the darkness. "There's still matters that need your attention."

"Couldn't I take care of those by fax or some other method? I've ran Fancy Duds for over five months in the same manner."

His gaze locked with hers. "I'm asking. Don't stay any longer than necessary, okay?"

Sorrow washed over her. How could she leave? Her mind grasped onto a thought. "Will you take good care of Tabacina and her kittens?"

"Sure. "He frowned. "You mean feed and water her. What do you mean, kittens? Is she....?"

Jessica looked away, focusing on her dressing table. "Didn't I mention that she was expecting?"

"No. When?"

She shrugged. "That's hard to say, since I don't keep up with her love life."

"I liked her better as a boy."

"Jason." She thumbed her smeared mascara.

A long silence passed before he finally answered. "Don't worry, I'll take care of her" His breath sounded loud in the darkened room. "Just give me your word that you'll come back."

She closed her eyes, knowing that she was saying good-bye one final time. "Tabacina only eats a certain type of cat food. I'll write the name on the kitchen note pad."

When the door closed, she lay back on the bed and let the tears flow unimpeded. Tomorrow she would book a flight, and for good, whether Jason knew it or not. She wouldn't return from Austin. Fancy Duds could easily afford the thirty thousand dollars she owed Jason for running the farm, even if it meant delaying the new line. Who cared about an inheritance? Her business was strong, even without the new venture into children's clothing.

Of course, she couldn't say the same about her heart. She'd never felt more vulnerable. But life would go on whether she wanted it to or not, and at the moment she didn't care.

Seventeen

The large jet set its cumbersome body down, light as a feather, as it landed on the runway of the Austin-Bergstrom International Airport that early evening in October. Jessica had been delivered back to the place she'd claimed as her home for the last eight years.

The plane rolled to a stop and once the seatbelt light went out she began gathering her things. In the terminal, she fought her way over to claim her baggage. She never ceased to be amazed by the way people's manners deserted them in a hurried situation like this, but she had learned to be as aggressive as the next person. If you had to live in the jungle, you needed to be able to hold your own with the animals.

Her luggage in her possession, she stepped out into

the still, warm evening and hailed a cab. Giving the driver the address, she climbed in and leaned back in the seat as the taxi pulled away from the terminal.

The capital of Texas was a lovely old city, hosting schools for the deaf and blind, the University of Texas—which Jessica had attended for four years—as well as the LBJ ranch just fifty miles to the west. The taxi passed the campus where she had spent long hours sitting in the large LBJ Library, cramming for tests with Barb and Ginny Lou, her closest friends throughout her college years. Ginny Lou had gone on to become an elementary school teacher, while Barb and Jessica launched Fancy Duds.

A smile curved her lips as she thought of all the good times they had had together—those late-night gab sessions in Jessica's room—Barb either in the clouds from her latest love or in the depths of dark despair from the lack of one. They consumed large quantities of Coke and potato chips, sitting in the middle of Jessica's bed, agonizing over Ginny Lou's unquestionable fate of forever being a bridesmaid but never a bride. At times Ginny Lou grew so desperate about the prospect of becoming an old maid she would wave the potato chip sack wildly over the bed before Jessica's distressed eyes. By the time the pair left for their own rooms, Jessica would have to drag out the little Dustbuster she kept in her closet and vacuum out her bed before going to sleep that night.

Nestled in the back seat of the taxi, Jessica indulged in an open laugh as she thought of her friend, now happily married and expecting a child any day.

The taxi pulled into the drive of Mrs. Houseman's house, a homey little bungalow with its flowers and shrubbery looking very peaceful in the gathering twilight. She'd often thought of buying a home of her own, or moving into an upscale apartment. She could certainly afford to. But somehow, she couldn't force herself to leave this place and its motherly owner. Jessica paid her cab fare, adding a generous tip as the driver removed her luggage from the trunk and set the suitcases on the drive. Jessica picked them up and walked around to the back of her landlady's house and rang the bell. Mrs. Houseman threw open the door. Upon catching sight of Jessica, she enveloped her in a maternal hug.

"I am so glad you're home. Things have not been the same around here," she complained. "I'd look up at your apartment every night, and there would be no lights on, and I'd have such a lonely feeling." She exhaled a wistful sigh "I've missed you something fierce. Why, I didn't have a soul to tell all my problems to."

Jessica hugged her affectionately. "There are a lot of people who would be more than happy to spend time talking with you." She dropped into a teasing tone. "How's Mr. Hawks?"

"Oh, my, Mr. Hawks, that old degenerate!" Mrs. Houseman became quite flustered. "Now, why in the world would I want him around underfoot?"

Jessica grinned mischievously. "I don't think he'd mind keeping you company in the evenings. Does he still just 'happen by' almost every night, anyway?"

"Oh, flitter, I can't seem to step out my back door that he doesn't show up, looking for a piece of that lemon cake he's always been so fond of." Smile lines wreathed her face.

"Well," Jessica replied tactfully, "it's a good thing you find time to bake a fresh one a couple of times a week, or he'd be up that proverbial creek without a paddle, wouldn't he?"

A pretty glow colored Mrs. Houseman's cheeks. "Let's just forget about Mr. Hawks for now." She hastened to change the subject. "Come on, I'll fix us a glass of fresh lemonade. I know you must be tired from your flight."

They stepped into the house. The large kitchen still held the smells of the fried chicken Mrs. Houseman had fixed for her dinner that evening. A covered plate sat on the table, still containing pieces of the golden-brown, crispy meat.

"If you're hungry, I'll fix you a plate. I know how you've always loved my chicken." She smiled proudly. "Just sit down and help yourself."

How could she resist the temptation? She reached for a fat drumstick, bit into the tender meat, and rolled her eyes up toward the ceiling. "This is fantastic. I don't know how you do it. I've tried fixing it just as you told me, and it doesn't taste nearly this good."

"Oh, it's just always a treat to eat someone else's cooking, dear, that's the only difference." She beamed, setting a plate with a blue willow design down in front of Jessica as she pushed a bowl of fresh green beans from her summer garden toward her. From the refrigerator, she retrieved a plate and uncovered a layer of Saran Wrap to reveal thick slices of juicy red tomatoes. "The tomatoes didn't do so well this year.". She put a slice on Jessica's plate. "The garden just dried up from lack of rain. I tried to water it, but it made my water bill run too high."

"I know," Jessica sympathized, munching on her chicken. "It was dry everywhere this year."

She ate the remainder of her dinner, engaging in pleasant small talk, with Mrs. Houseman hovering over her, offering her more than she could possibly eat.

When she'd didn't have room for one more bite, Jessica pushed back from the table, took her plate over to the sink and rinsed it. All her plants lay lovingly arranged on a table in front of one of the kitchen windows. Mrs. Houseman had been caring for them during her absence, and they all had such a green, healthy appearance—her tiny baby's tears was thick and full in its pot and the bridal veil bloomed in gay profusion. The large yellow "pocketbook" plant, as Jessica had always called it, had blossomed in glorious bright colors, its fat little "pocketbooks," speckled with red, hanging lightly on the stems. They glowed with the love Mrs. Houseman had given them.

"Mrs. Houseman," Jessica said suddenly, "would you mind keeping these plants permanently? I'm afraid if I move them now, they'll not do as well. I can always get new starts."

Mrs. Houseman's face lit up in a bright smile. "Why, I would love to keep them, if you're sure. I've become quite fond of them. They're almost like my children." She grinned sheepishly. "That philodendron and I have a long conversation over breakfast every morning."

Jessica smiled tenderly. "I couldn't think of a nicer home for them to 'grow up' in. Please take them with my blessings."

Mrs. Houseman crossed over to the plants and beamed down at them. "Well, now, see what I told you, children. Everything always has a way of working out for the best."

Jessica let herself into her dark apartment, reaching for the light switch as she set her bag inside the door. The three-room apartment came to life as the glow from the lamp flooded the small area. She crossed over to open the window, letting the fresh air in the stuffy room, and continued into her bedroom, where she turned on the bedside lamp and sank onto the bed. As she lay on her back looking up at the white ceiling and thinking of Jason, a deep sense of loneliness crept over her. He was nearly seven hundred miles away from her now. She closed her eyes, remembering the feel of his arms the night of the storm, and bit her lip to keep the tears from falling. That was a new, and unwelcome change in her. Until she had returned home for Aunt Rainey's funeral, she had never been one to burst into tears at the drop of a hat. She was a corporate executive, the one in control. But for the last few months it seemed all she had done was cry. How could a girl love someone so much and be so miserable?

The apartment was beginning to lose its musty smell as she sat up and moved to the corner of the bed. What she needed now was a hot shower and a good night's rest. She hadn't gotten over having just three hours of sleep the night before.

What is Jason doing now? Probably still working, either on his farm or hers. Guilt stabbed at her. Soon she'd have to tell him his services were no longer required, since the farm would belong to the church.

She set about unpacking the things she had brought with her. She would have to send for the rest of her belongings later.

When she stepped into the small blue-tiled bathroom for her shower, she released a long sigh. Loneliness ached in her chest. The next few weeks would be difficult. Work would help, of course. She could throw herself into making up for so much time away from the office. Since the children's clothing line was no longer possible, maybe she could develop a new marketing effort to expand the distribution—

Stop. I'm too tired to think about this tonight.

Instead, she closed her eyes, turned her face to the spray, and willed the hot water to wash away her thoughts. Especially thoughts of the green-eyed man she'd left behind.

Maybe tomorrow would be brighter.

Up bright and early the next morning, she dumped out a bowlful of the cornflakes Mrs. Houseman had sent over, poured the donated milk over them, and made herself a cup of instant coffee from the supplies still in her cabinet. Sitting at the table, she scooped a spoonful of cereal and thought of Jason. What was he having for breakfast this morning? Probably a piece of toast or something simple, since she wasn't there to cook a hearty meal for him.

Overwhelming sadness washed over her. How she longed to be back home with him right now.

With a sigh, she finished her simple meal, and then put the bowl and cup in the dishwasher. Someday, maybe, she would be able to think about something besides Jason Rawlings. It was going to be a long, long day.

She dressed in a pair of Fancy Duds jeans and pulled on a starchy white blouse and a Fancy Duds jacket. A check in the mirror revealed that CEO Jessica Cole had returned. With a final pat on her pinned-up hair, she let herself out of the apartment to go down to the garage directly below. She swung open the heavy door and saw her little red sports car sitting patiently waiting for its mistress to return.

"Boy, have I missed you," she assured it with a loving stroke on the back fender. "I've got a truck I want you to meet someday. You're not going to believe it."

She slid into the familiar seat, started the engine with no difficulty, backed slowly out of the garage. Mrs. Houseman appeared at the kitchen window to wave goodbye. Jessica returned the gesture and headed for work.

"You're back!" Celeste nearly bowled Jessica over when she entered the office. "Ohmygosh you have *no idea* how much we've missed you." She cast a cautious glance over her shoulder and lowered her voice. "If you'd been gone much longer, I think Louis was planning a *coup d' etat*."

Jessica laughed aloud at the outrageous idea. Louis, the mousy but brilliant manager of the computer room, was so shy he could barely talk to anyone without stammering and turning four shades of purple. Put him in front of a computer, though, and he could make the thing do back flips.

She hugged Celeste once more. "I'd worry more about you trying to take over than Louis," she teased before releasing her.

"Not me, boss lady." The perky girl placed a hand over her heart. "I'm sticking with you 'till death do us part."

The casual words might be lightly meant, but Jessica fought a stab of sorrow upon hearing them. She and Jason had made that promise to each other long ago. What would life have been like if she had kept it?

With a firm mental effort, she pushed thoughts of Jason out of her mind and headed toward her office behind Celeste's desk. "What's on my agenda for the day?"

"Are you kidding?" Celeste asked. "Nothing. We didn't know you were coming. Your calendar's completely empty."

All day long with nothing to do but think? Not happening.

"Well, fill it up. I want to meet with every department head, and tell them I want to see a summary of their activity over the past few months, as well as their current project lists. And this afternoon, book a couple of hours with the entire marketing team. I've got some ideas for a new campaign." She stopped in the act of opening the door with her name etched on the glass. "And as soon as Barb gets here, ask her to come in. We have a ton of catching up to do."

Celeste straightened to attention and gave a mock-salute. "Yes, ma'am, boss lady."

With a grin for her beloved assistant, Jessica entered her office.

She worked well past quitting time, reviewing every departments' status reports. By the time she pulled her car into the garage night had fallen. She slumped behind the wheel, tired from a full day of mental exertion.

Well I've used up one day of the rest of my life without Jason. A tight knot formed in her throat. One day. And it seemed like a week. How could she ever make it?

Grabbing her briefcase off the passenger seat, she climbed the stairs to her apartment. Inside, she went through the motions of readying herself for bed. She downed a glass of warm milk, like Aunt Rainey used to give her when she couldn't sleep. Then she crawled into bed.

And stared misty-eyed at the dark ceiling for the rest of the night.

Eighteen

The next few days blurred together. At the office Jessica worked like a fiend, throwing all her efforts into getting back up to speed. Though she hated to admit it, the company had run smoothly without her. Her staff was thrilled to have her back, and Barb couldn't stop hugging her, but the telecommuting arrangement did work out well.

When she left work, the problems began. Emotions overtook her at odd times, and it was not uncommon for her to burst into tears at the smallest thing. One evening she stopped at the local drugstore to buy a new paperback—anything to take up the empty hours of the endless lonely nights. The book selected, she browsed through a large display of cologne. Out of the corner of her eye she glimpsed the aftershave display. With faltering steps, she walked over slowly and picked up the dark amber bottle, holding it almost reverently. She removed the top of the bottle and inhaled deeply, breathing in the rich masculine scent...the one Jason wore. A river of tears coursed down her face as she stood cradling the aftershave, her hands trembling. Dragging a Kleenex out of her purse, she wiped her eyes and replaced the lid on the bottle. She started to put it back on the shelf, but paused. Her heart aching, she carried it to the check-out counter along with her book. It was a small comfort...but at least it was something.

She drove home with tears still in her eyes and let herself into the apartment just as her cell rang.

Jessica's heart leaped into her throat. *Please let it be him.* If only she could hear a deep manly voice begging her to return home. Instead she found herself explaining irritably to a persistent salesman that she didn't need aluminum siding for her house. She didn't have a house.

On the evening of the eighth day, Jessica stood at the window looking down into Mrs. Houseman's back yard, wreathed in shadows at the approaching twilight. Eight days. Had it been eight thousand she couldn't have been lonelier. She swallowed against a throat that threatened to clog with yet another lump of tears.

The dark sky began to take on a stormy appearance, the promise of much-needed rain hanging heavy in the sultry air. Thunder rolled in the distance. The faint scent of coming rain blew in the open window on a muggy breeze. Then a sharp streak of lightning lit up the sky as the storm overtook the city. A loud clap of thunder shook the small apartment. Jessica's pulse kicked into overdrive. Down in the yard, Mrs. House-man's webbed lawn chairs were blown by a strong gust, and smacked against her garage.

Irritation nagged at her. Her *empty* garage. An annoying incident with the car on the way home had left her without transportation for a few days. If only she'd—

No. She refused to think about that now. The night was depressing enough already.

The rumble of thunder reminded her of the night Jason comforted her.

Who was she kidding? Everything reminded her of Jason.

What is he doing right now?

Did he miss her even a tiny bit? Her chest heaved with a short laugh.

"Obviously not." Irony saturated the words, echoing off the apartment walls. No doubt he was glad to see the last of her. Probably enjoyed a return to sanity from the life he had led the last few months.

She pulled the window down a little before going to her bedroom. Before she drew the curtains, she glanced once more at the storm. Maybe it would just be a good rain this time instead of a true storm. She could hope, right?

Sliding between her sheets, she picked up the paperback from the nightstand tried unsuccessfully to concentrate on the hero and heroine. An hour later she tossed the book on the table in disgust. How could she expect to read about a man's undying love for his sweetheart and keep her mind off Jason? Next time she bought a book, she'd choose a science fiction novel. Surely an alien with stuff hanging out of his nose wouldn't stir her memory.

Switching off the bedside lamp, she settled down. Her muscles refused to relax as the sounds of the mounting fury of the storm invaded her bedroom. There was no doubt left in her mind now—it was clearly going to be a full-blown Texas-size storm. A good thing she'd exhausted herself at work today, or she'd be up all night worrying. But sleep lulled her to relax almost against her will. Snuggling deep under the covers, she drifted into a light slumber, one ear tuned to the wind, lest it take her roof off.

After only a few minutes, her subconscious mind registered a loud pounding. Refusing to emerge from her much-needed sleep, she snuggled deeper into her soft pillow. Probably a shudder or something banging in the wind.

The persistent noise became louder.

That wasn't a loose shudder. It sounded more like someone pounding on a door. Who would be visiting Mrs. Houseman at this hour? It sounded like that person was trying to beat the wooden door down with his bare hands.

"Jessica!"

Her mind swam to the surface. Wait. That was *her* door they were trying to beat down!

"Jessica, you'd better be in there." The howling wind outside muffled a man's deep voice.

She sat up, her heart pounding as she put her feet on the floor. Still groggy, she staggered into the front room and groped for the light switch. If this was Avon calling, they had gone berserk.

"I'm coming, I'm coming," she shouted, belting her housecoat around her waist. "Just hold on a minute."

She reached the protesting door, which was now groaning under the battering assault. Whoever it was, he was determined to get in. Fear assaulted her, and she stopped in the act of reaching for the security chain. What if it was a madman? This might be a home invasion!

Raising her voice to be heard over the banging and the wind, she demanded, "Who is it?"

"Who do you think it is? Open this door— NOW!"

Her heart soared to her throat. She knew that voice.

"Jason?" she asked in astonishment.

She quickly pulled the chain off and flung the door wide open. Warm rain blew in on her.

Maybe she was still asleep. This had to be a dream. Jason stood there in the doorway, his clothes plastered to his body. Rain ran in rivulets off the brim of his hat. When the door opened, his large frame sagged weakly against the doorframe. Fatigue lined his face, and heavy dark circles smudged his eyes.

He heaved a deep sigh. "It's about time. I was beginning to think you weren't home."

Her brain numb, she couldn't come up with a response to him. What was he doing here? Eight days had passed without a phone call, or a text, or even an email. No contact what so ever. Something must have gone wrong back at the farm.

"What's the matter? Is something wrong at home?" She studied his troubled face for a moment, then exclaimed, "It's Tabacina, isn't it? She's had her kittens."

Jason's jaw dropped. "Kittens? You think I flew seven hundred miles to tell you the cat had kittens?"

"She hasn't?" She shook her head to clear her thoughts. A lingering sleep clogged her brain. "She's really late."

"No, she hasn't." He moved his head, and a waterfall sloshed off the rim of his hat. "Do you think I could come in?"

"Oh. Of course." She opened the door wider and stepped back.

He brushed past her into the small living room. She shut the door, still trying to figure out what had brought him here in the middle of the night. A tiny drop of hope bubbled in her heart, but she ignored it.

She tried again. "Is there something wrong?"

He looked up in a daze, as if he were just now seeing her for the first time. Anger flickered in his jade eyes.

"Wrong?" He removed his hat and set it on the counter that separated the living room and kitchen. "Wrong, Jessica? Why, no, nothing's wrong. Not unless you consider my being stuck in an airport half the night last night trying to get here, then traipsing around this town in total confusion all day trying to find out where you lived, then spending the last two hours wandering around in this—this—monsoon looking for your address, as wrong." He began pacing the floor like a caged animal, his boots, which were filled with rainwater, sloshing with every step.

"But—but why are you here?" Jessica's pulse began to pound. The bubble of hope expanded.

"Why am I here?" He shouted the question. "That's what I came to ask you. Why are *you* still here?"

She looked away, unable to meet his penetrating gaze. "Where else do I belong?"

"With me. You belong with me. You told me you'd be back in a couple of days."

She stiffened and forced herself to meet his gaze. "I'm not coming back, Jason."

His lips tightened, and his eyes never left hers. "You wouldn't like to lay odds on that, would you, Cole?"

What is that supposed to mean? Is he determined to make me work out the full six months we agreed to?

Her chin threatened to tremble. "Why didn't you just let things alone? You don't love me. I'm in the way back home, a constant reminder of the pain of our annulled marriage." She began to pace the floor, following in Jason's footsteps.

"What do you mean, don't *love* you?" He whirled and passed her going the opposite direction. "Where did you get a stupid idea like that?"

She stopped in her tracks and jammed her small fists on her hips, her mouth dropping open. "A stupid idea like that?" She shot her nose in the air. "When have you ever told me you loved me? It's always been me dogging your steps ever since the first day I met you, you—you—you toad."

He stopped in front of her, his hands coming up sharply to his own hips. "I told you on our wedding night, you—you toadess!"

Every second of that night was emblazoned in Jessica's memory. "You did not. You said you wanted me. You said you loved my eyes, my nose, my face—"

"Wanted? Loved? What's the difference? Your eyes, your nose, your face—they're all you." Jason threw a hand in the air. "You know perfectly well I've never gotten you out of my system." Irritation filled his voice as he resumed pacing in a huff, bellowing above his squishing shoes. "Lord knows I tried—and I almost made it. Then you came back and set out to systematically destroy every means of transportation I own." He whirled sharply, his face inches from hers. "I'm surprised you didn't run over my horse."

She clenched her teeth, frustration washing over her as she doubled up her fists and shook them wildly in his face. "I'm sick of hearing about those stupid wrecks. I'll pay you back every penny. In fact, if my company's new promotion works out I'll buy you a car lot of your very own."

With a snort, he ignored her last remark. "Then you used our 'business arrangement' to try to seduce me."

She drew in an outraged breath. "I did not!"

"Oh?" One eyebrow twitched upward. "What was with the purple dress that almost dipped down to your navel?"

Heat assaulted her face. "That was unintentional. I didn't realize...I thought..." She straightened her shoulders and tried to gather a few shreds of dignity. "I wanted you to find me attractive. That's all."

"See!" He stabbed a finger in her face. "You purposefully tried to manipulate my feelings when you knew I hadn't gotten over you."

"You said you had." Jessica held firm to her argument. "You plainly told me the day I hired you that you didn't care for me any longer. Then, the night I gave you a harmless little peck on the cheek you went ballistic."

They both began their pacing again, passing each other in heated silence.

"And what about Monica?" She whirled on him in triumph. "Just explain why you've continued to see her all these months if you love me, Jason Rawlings."

"What about Rick? You threw him in my face enough in the last few weeks, Jessica Cole."

She dismissed that with a wave. "You know perfectly well I don't care for Rick romantically."

He snorted in disgust as he passed her. "It didn't look that way to me the night of the hayride."

"Yeah? Well from where I sat it looked like you and Monica were getting pretty cozy too."

Jason came to a stop. His muscles went limp, as if all the fight left him at once. "Do you honestly believe for one moment that I don't love you, Angel?"

Her anger fled just as quickly. She froze, barely able to breathe. "Oh, Jason, I want so desperately to believe that you do."

They stood in the middle of the small room staring at each other, the rain pattering against the windowpanes.

His muscular shoulders lifted in a slight shrug. "You can believe it, or not. I'm tired of fighting. I want you to come home with me." His throat moved as he swallowed. "I—I love you and I want you. If I can't have it all, then I'll take what I can."

The words fell on her ears like feathers, soft and caressing. Did he really just say that? Could he *really* love her?

"Why would you think that you couldn't have it all?" she whispered. "I've always been yours."

The green eyes darkened. "Then why were you able to give me up so easily eight years ago?" Pain flooded his tone.

Tears blurred her vision. "Easily? Is that what you think?" A lump lodged in her throat. "You'll never know how many times I wanted to call you those few days before I left for college. I desperately wanted to beg you to come for me." She averted her eyes, unable to watch the torture in his face. "I felt like I owed Uncle Fred and Aunt Rainey their dream that I go to college. I—I was so young. I know that's no excuse, but..." She took a step toward him, and extended a hand to hover in the air between them. For the first time in eight years, she spoke without thinking, letting her heart utter the words she'd wanted to tell him for almost a decade. "If I could put back the hands of the clock—and, Jason, I'd give my life to—then there would be no power on earth that could separate me from you. Don't you know I've loved you from the first day I set eyes on you? I know I've hurt you, but believe me, my pain is as great as yours." She poured as much emotion into her words as she could dredge from the bottom of her soul. "I love you beyond belief. Please believe me."

In the next instant, the distance between them dissolved. With two long-legged strides, Jason swept her into his arms and pulled her close to his chest. Jessica breathed in the manly scent of him and buried her face in his shirt.

"I thought I'd never hear you say those words, Angel." His whisper came out ragged, stark with emotion. "I'm sorry for what I've put you through."

"Shhh-shhh." Jessica looked up to lay a finger over his lips.

Ever so gently, he removed her hand and entwined his fingers in hers. "No, let me say this—I love you, Jessica Cole. I love you."

The bubble of hope burst, flooding her heart with

joy. *He loves me!*

She tilted her head to assure him again of her deep and abiding love, but the words died when she was swept up in his emerald gaze. Slowly, deliberately, without looking away from her, Jason's head descended toward hers. Jessica slid a hand up his wet chest and around his neck, and sank her fingers into his thick, damp curls. In the moments before their lips touched, she breathed deeply, inhaling his warm breath.

And then she was swept away to another world, a world where nothing existed but her and the man she loved, their mouths locked in a kiss that rocked her to the soles of her feet. An eternity passed while she poured eight years' worth of unexpressed love into her kiss.

Finally, he ended the embrace. "Whoa, there, Angel. We'd best put the skids on this before things get out of hand."

The 'bad girl Jessica' did a quick battle with the 'good girl Jessica.' Thank goodness Jason possessed more self-control than she did. Reluctantly, she loosened her hold on him.

"I hope that kiss was a wedding proposal," she teased. "Because if not, I'm about to sink down on one knee and pop the question myself."

He threw back his head, and his joyful laugh echoed in the small room. "Consider yourself proposed to, Cole. In fact, the sooner the better. I want us to go back home as Mr. and Mrs. Rawlings. Can we make that happen ASAP?"

She smiled. "You bet I can."

Nineteen

Though thrilled to meet Jessica's new fiancée, Mrs. Houseman apparently felt it her duty to act as chaperone in the two days before their hastily-arranged second wedding. She offered Jason the guest room in her house, conveniently located next door to hers. Jessica giggled at the consternation in his face as he accepted what was clearly not a mere suggestion.

Though it rained over the next two days, the morning of their wedding dawned bright and glorious. Jessica had insisted on a private event, but how could she exclude Barb and Celeste? Before she knew it, word had spread through the Fancy Duds factory, and the guest list came close to fifty.

Throughout the morning, Jessica kept peering

through the windows at Mrs. Houseman's glorious back yard. The rain had greened everything up nicely, and flowering hedges bordered the small space behind the comfortable house.

"Are you ready for this?" Barb asked as she twitched at a fold in Jessica's skirt—a Fancy Duds denim with an elaborate sequined design, naturally.

Jessica found it hard to contain her grin. "Honestly? Readier than for anything in my entire life."

Barb swept her in a hug. "I'm so happy for you, girl. But how are we going to manage without you here every day?"

"You will," Jessica promised. "And I promise to fly here one week every month. After all, we're going to have a new children's designer line to launch!"

They grinned at one another. Then Ginny Lou, her belly round with child, stuck her head in the door. "The minister's here. Are you ready?"

A flutter started in Jessica's heart. "Am I ever!" She started to race toward the door.

Barb grabbed her by the crook of her arm. "Hold up, girl. You don't want to look too eager."

Jessica couldn't manage to dismiss the grin from her face. "Why not? This is the best day of my life."

Together, the three friends descended the stairs to the back yard...to Jessica's future.

∞

"Do you, Jason Rawlings, take this woman, Jessica Rainey Cole, to be your lawfully wedded wife?"

Jessica barely managed to focus on the minister's words as he rattled on about having and holding, so caught up was she in Jason's green gaze.

When he spoke, his voice held a solemn finality that set her heart fluttering.

"I do."

The minister turned to her. "And do you, Jessica Rainey Cole, take this man..."

The words blurred as Jessica lost herself in her husband's eyes. Her *true* husband. He'd been that since the first time they took these vows.

Now came the time for her to promise. She'd one it once before, and then broke her word.

"...until death do you part?"

Jessica held Jason's shining green gaze.

"Even longer—if that's permissible."

The soft patter of rain falling on the roof made a melodious backdrop for the two lovers. The ceremony over, the friends greeted, the gifts opened. Jessica and Jason had celebrated their wedding with their friends in a manner neither of them would soon forget.

Jason unlocked the door of her apartment, and then turned to sweep her up into his arms.

"Tradition, right?" He grinned.

"Absolutely, Sir Toad."

She was swept across the threshold and into the apartment where she'd spent so many lonely days.

But never again.

He set her down in the living room and captured her lips with his. Once again Jessica was caught up in an emotional heaven.

Finally, he lifted his head. Holding her hand close to his lips, he kissed the tip of each finger, whispering, "Mrs.—Jason—Rawlings—Jessica—Rawlings. Has a nice ring to it, doesn't it?"

Delight swept through her. "Oh, yes."

"I love you, Angel."

Jessica raised her face to his. "Now, that really has a nice ring to it."

"I love you, I love you, I love you," Jason whispered

over and over in her ear.

She splayed fingers, admiring the wedding ring that she'd saved from eight years before. How could she get rid of it, when it had been a gift from the only man she would ever love?

"When we get back home, I'll buy you a diamond the size of Texas," he promised.

She laughed. "I don't want it. This ring is perfect." Nuzzling into the delectable curve where his neck met his shoulder, she whispered, "And since we're married, you can have all my money to do with as you wish."

A low rumble of laughter came from Jason's throat as he smoothed her dark hair back from her face. "I don't need your money, sweetheart."

"But you're welcome to it," Jessica insisted. "You've nearly killed yourself the last few months working both farms."

Pulling her head closer, he whispered in her ear, "I guess that was my way of telling you I loved you— every day for the last five months. I needed another thirty thousand dollars like I needed another day's work."

Jessica drew back, giving him a puzzled look.

"Honey, listen to me." He put a hand on each of her arms. "Just before my dad died, they found oil on the five hundred acres he owned in Dallas. It made us all millionaires. Eric stays up there and runs the business for us because I wanted to work the farm." His hands slid up to her shoulders. "Jessica, I've got enough money to burn a wet mule. So, every day I ran that farm for you was a labor of love. I was doing it because I loved you and couldn't let you walk back out of my life again. Do you understand?"

Jessica brought her hands up, running her fingers along his smoothly shaven jaw, her eyes shining with love. "Yes, my darling Jason. I believe you and—thank you." She wrapped her arms around his neck and hugged him tightly,

"You're more than welcome, Angel."

They kissed tenderly, savoring the sweetness of the moment.

"I—can I ask one more thing?" She dredged up the question that had clouded her mind the past few days. "About Monica... Did you—well—did you love her?"

He paused for a moment. "Honestly, I tried to. I wanted to. And maybe there was a time when I thought I did, but I think she knew all along how I felt about you." He put a finger under her chin and lifted her face toward his. "She is really a nice person, Jessica, but it's you I love. I told her just before I flew down here, and she understood."

Jessica had to fight the urge to do a cartwheel. "Finally, Jason Rawlings loves Jessica Cole!" She showered his face with a multitude of feather kisses, lulling him into a peaceful glow.

Laughing, he grasped her wrists and wrestled her arms down to her sides. "Right now, Angel, I think we need some sleep. We have a long trip ahead of us in the morning."

She indulged in a tiny frown. "Uh—Jason... I have something to tell you."

His eyebrows cocked to attention. "Yes?"

"Uh, you know I have a car. She's a sweet little sports car and I love her."

"Okay, sweetheart." He grinned. "Will you let me drive her? We can ride home together instead of flying."

"Well..." She paused, hesitant to confess the last secret she had kept from him. "There's just one small thing."

"What's that, honey?"

She backed up and allowed her agitation over the incident to show. "Jason, you're not going to believe this, but on the way to the market the other day, some idiot pulled out in front of me, and—."

One large hand reached out to cover her mouth.

"It's okay," he reassured her. "After all, you're going to buy me a car lot, right?"

Laughing, Jessica threw her arms around his neck and pulled him close for another kiss, confident that this one would last forever.

A Note from Lori

I began my publishing journey long ago. When my first few books were published, I thanked God for the opportunity and then followed the guidance of a series of editors employed by large publishing houses. After a while, I felt an unmistakable nudge from the Lord—He wanted me to write books that honor Him, and some of my work didn't. He directed me to a Christian publisher, and from that time until now I'm pleased to say God is honored in every book I write.

Some of those old books are still floating around. If I could buy up every tattered copy in every used bookstore and yard sale across the world, I would. Alas, that's an impossible task. I cringe to think my precious readers might stumble across one of them.

But even though I blush at some of the content, I love the characters. Since I can't obliterate the old books, at least I can redeem the stories. That's what I've done with *The Cowboy's Housekeeper*. This story was my very first published novel, and to this day I love Jessica and Jason. What a pleasure it has been to turn their book into a wholesome, clean romance that I'm proud to show my readers. I hope you enjoyed reading it as much as I did re-writing it.

About Lori

Lori lives in the beautiful Ozarks with her husband, Lance. Lance and Lori have three sons, three daughters-in-law, six wonderful grandchildren, and two great-granddaughters.

Lori began her writing career in 1982, writing for the secular book market. In 1999, after many years of writing, Lori sensed God calling her to use her gift of writing to honor Him. It was at that time that Lori began writing for the Christian book market.

Lori is the author of more than 100 titles, both historical and contemporary fiction. She has developed a loyal following among her rapidly growing fans in the inspirational market. She has been honored with the Romantic Times Reviewer's Choice Award, The Holt Medallion, and Walden Books' Best Seller award. In 2000, Lori was inducted into the Missouri Writers Hall of Fame.

Lance and Lori are very involved in their church, and active in supporting mission work through *School to the Nations*.

Love a good mystery?
Don't miss these!

Three generations of women under one roof.
All they want is to live a harmonious life in
the small town of Morning Shade. The last
thing they need is a mystery!

The **Diamonds in the Rough** Series

Bad Taste
Crooked Letters
Nosy Neighbors

CPSIA information can be obtained
at www.ICGtesting.com
Printed in the USA
LVOW07s2341030817
543783LV00001B/133/P